It's hard to miss the big body of Matthew when he's in motion and that he was, running down the boardwalk toward the gunfire. It was he that stopped the man dead in his tracks with his Winchester. Matthew was one of those people who didn't like wasting ammunition either.

The one shot I was able to get off in that split second was the one that lifted the third of Watts' gunmen up, pushing him back into a horse that kicked him before he fell. I doubt he ever felt the kick.

"Smart ass," I muttered, levering another round into my Brass Boy. . . .

THE
BRASS BOY

Jim Miller

FAWCETT GOLD MEDAL • NEW YORK

This one is for
George Bush, for his
cover art.

Chapter 1

The war was over. Or so they said.

You damn sure couldn't have proved it by the sour looks of the men standing at the bar I was leaning against. Men, hell! Half of them were only boys who'd aged too fast and just looked like men. Seen it before, you know.

The scruffy looking fellow next to me was the one I was talking to, but I had my back to the bar and my eyes on the rest of the saloon patrons as I did my palavering with him. You see, we were in the heart of Texas right then, and from all I'd heard the last year or so, why, these Texican lads didn't take kindly to losing. None of those Confederate boys did. One man hit the nail on the head when he came up with his own version of one of those back east sayings: *It matters not whether you win or lose . . . until you lose*. If you know what I mean.

"Say you can cook, huh?" Like I said, I was watching the crowd as I spoke. Besides, this fellow next to me was just too ugly to look at all that long.

"You betcha, Black Jack!" I figured him for one of these Texicans all right. Some of his words dragged out longer than others, even when he was in a hurry, but I paid little mind to it. Hell, ain't nobody's got an accent until he leaves home and wanders into someone else's pastures.

"Coffee very hour of the day, thick enough to eat with a spoon if you ain't got your cup handy. Sourdoughs that're right tasty, hot or cold. Beans, three different pies, and anything else your supply wagon's carrying." He was smiling through three weeks' growth of whiskers, but it still didn't do an awful lot for his looks. Ask me, someone who wasn't too satisfied with his cooking once took the bottom end of the skillet to this fellow's face.

"What about meat?" I said, cocking a suspicious eye at him. "You ain't said nothing 'bout that."

"You supply me the meat and I'll cook it any way you want it." He wasn't lacking any confidence, I'll say that for him. "Young steer's good for sonofabitch stew, although I ain't too keen on some of them wild turkeys . . ."

He kept on palavering about how he could make a jack rabbit stretch for near a dozen men and some other such miracles that I could only remember being performed before in the Good Book, but I didn't hear the half of it. My attention had turned to my two boys.

Matthew, he's the oldest of the two; thirty and some in age and a bit bigger than me in build and height. Hold his own any day of the week, he could. He'd been sitting at one of the tables as the two of us waited for his younger brother, Jedediah. I figured it would be some kind of reunion since the boys hadn't seen one another in three, maybe four years. Matthew—everyone except me calls him "Guns" because of the passion he's always had for firearms—had reached his full growth and was a big, tall, lean man. I'd run into Diah a few days back and found that he'd filled out a good deal as well since I'd last seen him a couple of years before.

Diah, that's short for Jedediah, was a decade and some younger than his brother. The last time Matthew had seen him, he'd been tall but skinny. Us Hookers have a tall branch in the family tree. Jedediah Strong Smith Hooker was Diah's full name. I'd given him that moniker out of a great respect for a mountain man I'd known only briefly, but who was one of the bravest men I ever met. Matthew and me, we were always joshing the boy about that name. Diah never did like it, but he took it as good-naturedly as possible.

"Who's that?" the cook asked. Diah had walked into the saloon and just stood there while his eyes adjusted to the darkness. It was long enough to get the attention of most of the folks in the saloon, him standing just inside the batwings, the silhouette of his six-foot frame outlined in the entrance.

"My boy," I said with a good bit of pride. Somehow I reckon a father never does get tired of saying those words that way.

"Do tell."

It was the moment I'd been waiting for. I'd brought my boys together for the first time in three or four years. I envisioned them shaking hands and giving one another a smile. Yes, sir, that I did.

"Filled out some, little brother," I heard Matthew say while Diah was adjusting to the dimness.

"That's a fact," Diah replied, speaking more to the voice than the man himself. Then he was looking at Matthew's table, seeing that mischievous smile his older brother had on.

"You done anything heroic since the last time I seen you, Diah?" Matthew said, still smiling. "Something along the lines of old Jed Smith, maybe?"

I don't think anyone was expecting it. I know I wasn't. And the way Matthew went flying ass over tea kettle when his brother hit him, well, he hadn't been expecting it either!

"Who's that he hit?" the fellow next to me said.

"My boy," I replied, only this time there was a scowl on my face as I moved toward them.

"What the hell did you do that for!" Matthew was rubbing his jaw as he got up. Except he never made it. He was on his knees just about to set one foot in place when Diah hit him again, knocking him back down to the floor. I don't think Matthew was expecting that either. I know I wasn't.

A couple of the bar patrons took to mumbling something off to my side as I made it to the upturned table.

Complaining about the drinks, likely. But at the moment I had a bit more serious situation in hand. I couldn't recall the last time I'd seen as much anger in Diah's eyes as he had now. As for Matthew, I only needed to give him one glance to know that the look on his face was the one that said "That tore it!" He was getting ready for war!

Some reunion.

"You just hold it right there, Matthew," I said, stepping as near to between them as I could. My oldest was now on his feet facing his brother. By the looks of them you'd think they were going to start the whole War Between the States all over again without either army.

"Diah," I said, no longer feeling pride swell up in me as I spoke the boy's name, "just what in thunder is going on here?"

"Don't ever say that to me again," the boy said, taking in the two of us. "That bit about Jed Smith. Don't *ever* say that to me again, understand?" Hard, cold, and dangerous, that's how it came out of him.

"Son, do you know who you're talking to?" I asked, just in case he'd lit into a bottle of Taos Lightning or some such, before I started taking him apart. Hell, you wouldn't let your youngsters sass you like that, would you?

"I know *exactly* who I'm talking to." Sober as a judge, he was, but that fire was still burning in him. Now, hoss, that got me interested. It also near got me killed.

There I was, so involved in what my sons were fighting about that I'd forgotten I was facing a wall with all of those angry Texicans behind me. Two things struck me at about the same time. The first was the thought that maybe that mumbling I'd heard when I left the bar wasn't complaining at all. Maybe it was a couple of lads sounding off who didn't care for Yankees, who hadn't called a truce to the war. The second thing that hit me was that ham hock Matthew calls a fist. I reckon that's what hit me the hardest.

He laid it into me at just about belt level with enough

force to bring the top half of me down right quick. I could faintly hear a pistol going off to my rear as my hat flew off the top of my head and Matthew bowled me over into the upturned table he'd been sitting at. Between Matthew's fist and the hard wood, well, I wasn't feeling any too feisty at the moment. Still, my rifle was on the floor and as soon as I got to it I was going to join in the shooting, whatever the hell was going on. Then I was going to beat the bejesus out of both my sons. Pride, my ass! Pain is what they were causing me!

A second shot had been fired as I fell, and I thought I recognized it as coming from that Spencer Diah carried. I was pushing Matthew away from me when I heard the action of Diah's rifle jacking another shell into the chamber. Out of the corner of my eye I could see him aiming it at someone across the room, a wisp of gunsmoke still trailing from the end of the barrel.

"It's your move, mister. Your friend ain't gonna try that again. It's up to you now." I didn't need to see Diah's face to know that his look was as hard and cold as his voice.

As silent as it had gotten I had the feeling that Matthew and I were the only ones moving. Not that I was any too quick getting up, you understand. I do believe I could've drunk a whole bottle of Taos Lightning then and there, my stomach needed that much settling.

The climate inside that saloon had changed quite a bit since I'd gone to palavering with my boys. I picked up my rifle, which I call Mister Henry, and sloshed on my hat, all the time keeping a wary eye on these Texicans, damn near every one of which was now on his feet, hand on a pistol butt. Diah had taken aim at one of the two I'd heard mumbling when I got into the argument between my boys. He'd positioned himself more toward the back of the room now. I'll tell you something else, hoss, that sweat he was carrying on his forehead didn't come from busting any broncs! Likely because he was plenty worried. Diah had been right. This man's partner had ceased having a future about a minute ago, laid out on the floor like he was.

"That wasn't a smart thing to do, friend," one of the other men said. Didn't sound none too friendly the way he said it either.

Diah didn't budge. "Trying to kill my pa wasn't any too bright on your friend's part either." There must've been a good fifteen of them standing there ready to go to war, and Diah was willing to take them to the wall all by himself. Like I said, sometimes you feel that bit of pride swell up in you.

"Don't do a thing, mister." Latch Key, the scruffy fellow I'd been talking to at the bar before this all started, had produced a pistol of his own and was now pointing it at the barkeep. "I want to see how this turns out." You'd have to have your brains falling out your ears not to know that the man behind the bar was reaching for a weapon of some sort. After all, he was in charge of the place.

"Don't be a fool, sonny," the tough-talking one said. "We've got you outgunned four ways from Sunday."

He was probably right because some of these lads were packing enough hardware to open their own armory. Not that you could really blame them. Hell, these carpetbaggers that had invaded the South after the war were none too welcome. Fact is, Yankees in general were none too welcome. Still, nobody likes being talked to like that. Diah stood his ground, never moving a muscle. Matthew snatched up that old Sharps of his and held it against his hip, ready to take out anyone who got in his way. Me, I flipped that fancy ring lever I'd had made on Mister Henry some time ago and cocked an eye at the crowd just to let them know I was feeling as gamey as they were.

"I don't know what day of the week it is, señor, but you may never reach Sunday," a voice with a Mexican accent said from the back of the room. When he spoke, he slurred some of the words in the way that a man does who hasn't gotten fluent in another man's language. The fellow standing next to him had a grin just as wide as his, and even looked a mite like him. But what they said and how they looked didn't get near as much attention from the Texicans who glanced over their shoulders at them as the fact that each of the Mexicans was holding two pistols. If all that bluster wasn't bluff, why, we'd evened up the odds considerable. Yes, I do believe we had.

"You're hired," I said to Latch Key. "Ary you can make food as well as you make use of that gun, I can use you."

"Obliged." The cook smiled, still standing there, still holding the business end of that Remington of his trained on the barkeep.

"Don't even think about it, son," Matthew said to some young buck in front of him. He had that eager look, the boy did, one that said he was looking to make a name for himself. But he wouldn't do so today. "Even if I missed you with this Sharps, the concussion would kill you," Matthew added. The boy backed water, a flushed look coming to his face. Seeing Matthew's crooked grin didn't help him any either.

"You fellas back out that door you came in and I'll buy you a drink at the edge of town," I bellowed to the two in the rear.

"Gracias." Lickity split and they were gone.

"Do you know who we work for?" the yahoo who'd taken over as spokesman for the Texans said.

"Nope," I replied. "Don't care neither. You boys just take your seats and that bear behind the bar will bring you a drink on the house." I had a feeling the storm had passed and I was right. There were still four guns in view that could tear the living hell out of these boys and that never appealed to any one that I know of.

Backing out of that saloon was a slow process. Not that we were being all that cautious, you understand. It was just that, well, I was still hurting some from busted wood and Matthew's knuckles. If you know what I mean.

"Say, wait a minute!" The big barkeep was working his way down the bar toward us, Latch Key right behind him, gun in hand. "Who's paying for the damages?"

"Them!" I said with as much force as I could muster

without feeling like the bottom half of me was going to fall off. "We didn't start it!"

He glowered at me as he bent over the bar and spoke in all but a hiss. "How in hell do you think I'm gonna collect from that bunch? Why, I'd be crazy to try to get any money off of them!"

"Dealing with them may be crazy, mister, but I guarantee that if you try collecting from me, you're gonna get one whale of a lesson in what the word *insane* means." I could hiss just as well as he could, and I imagine to all those young bucks sitting there it looked like a couple of old bulls going at it head to head. It must have been what was needed to break the tension for I heard several of them laugh while I left the place. That barkeep, well, he was doing a lot of cussing.

"Wanta think about hiring those fellas that come in the back door?" I said when we were a good block away from the saloon.

"I already did," Diah said. Whatever burr had crawled under his saddle, I had a notion it was going to take up residence there a while. You bet.

"I don't suppose you'd mind telling me—"

"Maybe someday, Pa, but I got things to do now," was all he said before he left. Sometimes Jedediah could be a puzzle.

"That being the case," I said, facing Matthew, "maybe you'd like to explain why the devil you laid me out that hard and fast." Not that I ever *demanded* anything from anyone, but my boys knew that when I asked a question, by God, I wanted an answer—or else. Diah must've known I wasn't in any condition to chase after him and took off. But I had the oldest one backed up against a wall now.

"You really want to know?" He had confidence, I'll say that for Matthew. But then, he always does.

"Of course I do, you—"

Before I could finish he'd grabbed my beaver pelt hat from my head and held it before me. In the rear the brim had a hole in it, freshly torn. Seeing it gave me the eerie feeling that if I went back to that saloon and looked close,

I'd find a slug in that front wall that would match the size of the hole in my hat. Then I realized that if my boy hadn't done what he had I'd likely be lying there back shot instead of just feeling busted up. Didn't make me feel any the better as far as pain went. But I'll tell you, hoss, it sure was nice knowing that I'd gotten away from Ezekiel's claw one more time.

"Oh," was all I said before putting the hat back on.

Shoot, boy, you didn't think I was going to apologize to my own son, did you?

Chapter 2

I knew who that bunch we'd tangled with was before we got to the edge of town. Matthew made sure of that.

"Most of 'em belong to Jared Watts," he said with a bit of concern in his voice.

"Do tell. Reckon I'll have to pay *Mister* Watts a visit soon. Did those two plug uglies that started the fandango look like they belonged to him?"

Matthew smiled. "Only by their actions that I know of."

Jared Watts was my competition. At least he had been my competition. Right now he was acting more like a sore loser than anything else. Like I said, these fellows down here take losing—at anything—real hard.

Driving a bunch of stubborn, bull-headed longhorns up the trail to Sedalia, Missouri, is what it was all about. The war being over and all, there was one hell of a shortage of beef in the East. All those hungry lads coming home from the war, I reckon. And wouldn't you know that when the Texas boys came home, why, they had a ready-made market for beef waiting for them.

All you had to do was ferret those longhorns out of the brush—no easy job by any means—and get them to market. Next thing you knew you could be rich. Or dead.

Word had it that a man by the name of Charlie Good-night and his partner, Oliver Loving, were heading west across Texas into New Mexico, seeing if they could find a good trail and a market at the end. Unless I missed my guess, they'd wind up at Fort Sumner and sell their beef at a good price, but it would be one hellacious trip, I'll guarantee you that, friend. Heat. Indians. Flat land that likely ain't seen water since Noah unloaded the Ark— and never will!

Me and my boys were doing the same thing, only we were headed north on what was being called the Shawnee Trail. It wound up in Sedalia, Missouri, where we'd sell our herd and ride back here to Texas with all that money. You see, hoss, the money wasn't all ours to keep.

It was me that first got the idea to give this a try. Diah, he was bankrolling the whole operation—wagons, cooking gear, and supplies, the whole shebang. He ran into some money out in Denver, he said. Got it from a marshal friend of his. I disremember his name. Matthew, he was just around. He always was.

Actually, it was him I had set to scouting out this Jared Watts and his crew. That was how he'd come to know so much about them. Watts owned a small spread, and I mean small. He barely had enough longhorns to call them a herd. Wasn't growing anything either. Now, hoss, you explain to me how a man who ain't doing much of anything on his spread can afford—or need— over a dozen men to work for him without being just a mite shady, and I'll eat my hat, beaver skin and all!

It seemed the whole countryside was peppered with small ranchers and cattlemen, men who were making a new start after the war. Every one of them was taking to brush popping, seeing if they couldn't scare up just one more maverick longhorn. What most of them had done that spring was band together to see if they couldn't get someone to take their herds north for them while they tended to the ranching back home. Hell, you wouldn't want to leave everything you had and come back only to find that some carpetbagger had taken it over or that the Comanches had burned it to the ground, would you?

Well, these smaller ranchers knew better than that, which is how I heard they were looking for someone who could put together a crew and drive some four thousand head of cattle up north to market. That's when I ran into Matthew and Diah separately and figured we could all make some money on this venture. After all, each of those ranchers was willing to pay a handsome price to have someone else make his profit for him.

Not that we were out to make enough to start our own spread, like some were. Hell, you wouldn't find many Hookers settled down anywhere. I reckon we were sort of like some of those Plains Indians, wandering here and there with the seasons. But as long as they paid it out in gold coin, money was money to me.

What made Jared Watts my *former* competition was the fact that, well, he wasn't really any competition to begin with. Oh, he'd snorted and stomped about like some bull about to charge, but it didn't take much to see that those ranchers wanted to be sure they got some money back from the meat on the hoof they were sending north to market. Like I said, Watts wasn't running nothing but gunmen on his range, and that in itself made a body wonder. What galled him was the fact that those little ranchers had stood up to him and chosen me, an outsider, over him to get those longhorns to Sedalia. It was as much as telling the man that they knew exactly what he was and that they didn't trust him with their cattle or their money. No, sir, Jared Watts had no love for me or mine.

"Any idea what got into Diah?" Matthew asked shortly, interrupting my thoughts. "He sure has gotten brassy since I saw him last."

"Lost his sense of humor, too, you ask me." The pain from my oldest son's fist was still playing havoc on my stomach, but it was the total obfuscation of what my youngest boy had done in that saloon that was really gnawing at my gut. "I don't know, son, I don't know. Let's just hope he don't keep it up."

The two Mexican pistoleros had taken me up on that

drink. They were leaning against the cottonwood we'd
made camp under and called home.

"How do, boys," I said as Matthew and I dismounted.

"Buenos dios," each said, almost together. But then,
I had a notion these two likely did most everything
together. "You made an offer of a drink?"

"You betcha." It was all I needed to say for Matthew
to go hunting up the tequila bottle. In the meantime I
gave a sideward glance at the mounts grazing nearby.
"These your cayuses, boys?"

"Si. Why do you ask?" From the tone of it I was
getting another notion about these two; that they had a
past—and maybe a wanted poster—that they weren't
too awful keen to palaver about. All of which was fine
with me. Hell, some of those boys I'd started out with
back when we were trapping the Shinin' Mountains never
did talk much about where they came from either. I
reckon as long as your past didn't catch up with you,
you're all right.

"Oh, nothing, son," I said, addressing the one who'd
spoken. "Just wondering why they wasn't swaybacked,
with as much artillery as you're packing."

That sort of broke the ice, although I'll be damned if I
know how you'd find ice in that place, as far gone as
spring was at the time. Fact is, I don't doubt that the
Almighty had started summer in the very territory we
were in and spread it out across the land, the days had
been that hot. When Matthew gave the Mexicans the
tequila bottle, each took a long swig like it was some
sort of soda pop they were drinking. That or they'd been
weaned on the stuff, which wasn't entirely out of the
question.

"I'm Guns Hooker," Matthew said, although I doubt
he had much interest in the men themselves at the moment. "Nice-looking Remingtons you got there." Like I
said, everyone else calls him Guns but me. "Mind if I
take a look?" he asked.

I took in our two new hired hands more fully while
Matthew surveyed the pistol the closer one handed to
him. Both wore the wide-brimmed sombrero of their

land, boots that were handmade and worn, and trousers
and shirts to match. Nothing fancy, you understand, but
you'd still have thought they were headed for some
fandango. Come to think of it, they'd just come from one!
A rawhide vest covered the shirts, with a bandolier of
rifle ammunition crossing each shoulder. Yes, sir, I do
believe these boys were ready for war. Oh, they were
lightweights to be sure; the tops of their sombreros
broke even with my chin. But with as much powder,
ball, casings, and lead as they were carrying, why, I'd
bet they had to eat beef steak three meals a day just to
keep up the strength to carry it all!

"Carry that much ammunition, why, a body'd think
you'd been fighting that Maximilian fella down south." I
flashed them a smile as I said it, but the two simply gave
one another confused looks.

"No, señor, you are mistaken," the closer one said.
Sort of a weak grin came along with the words.

"I see."

"Don't worry, Pa," Matthew said, hefting the pistol,
a mischievous smile coming to his face. "Anyone hands
over a handgun as free as this fella ain't likely to have
been much of anywhere." He twirled the gun around
once, bringing it to full cock when it was seated in his
palm, pointing right at the man who'd handed it to him.
Like I said, my oldest boy has always picked up on guns
right quick.

"You don't want to do that, señor," the other pistolero
said. The same sort of smile was spreading across his
face as Matthew was wearing. Slowly the Mexican with-
drew his wide-brimmed hat, revealing a cocked and ready
to fire pistol of his own. "I get along much better with
my brother than you do with yours."

A strange thing happened then, something I didn't
often see.

"I reckon you do, *amigo*," Matthew said. The two
men stood holding the guns on each other a moment
longer. But then my boy let the hammer down easy and
returned the Remington to the man he'd taken it from.
By the look of both of them I didn't figure there was

going to be any trouble. I'd only seen Matthew back off like this a couple of times, but it was his way of showing he'd accepted the man—in this case, men.

"Guns Hooker." The two shook hands.

"Juarez," the other said, "both of us. I am"—he hesitated a moment, caution suddenly upon him—"Bud. Yes. And this is my *hermano,* my brother, Jorge."

This just seemed to be another example of how it was getting so you couldn't tell if the man you were talking to would have been called the monicker he gave you by his own mama or not. Damn near everyone coming out here had some kind of a past he was running from. Or a future he was looking for. But you never could tell who was really who. The Mexican before me, well, Jorge might have been his brother's name, but he wasn't any "Bud" by a long shot.

"Least he done something right today." Saying it got me a few confused looks. "Diah, my boy. Said he took you on."

"Oh, *si,*" Bud, or whatever his name was, commented. "A fine young man." All smiles.

"Can you handle a rope and a horse as good as you do them guns?" Matthew asked, now serious.

"*Si,*" Bud said, still confident. "I will tell you stories on the way of how it was before the *norteamericanos* arrived. Yes, we can do all of that."

"That being the case, I only got one question," I said, looking them straight in the eye. "Why you signing on?"

The two looked at one another, shrugged, and this time it was Jorge who spoke. His voice was froggy sounding, as though he'd been kicked in the throat and most of the cider drained out of his Adam's apple.

"You are headed north?"

"That's the general idee," I said, cocking a suspicious eye at him.

"That is enough to know. That is the reason."

"Better'n most. Now where's that bottle of tequila?" I said.

Chapter 3

"Either one of you see where Latch Key went?"

"Who the hell's that?" Matthew asked.

A good swallow of that tequila had settled my innards some and these two Juarez lads and my boy had finished off the small amount left in the bottle. But the day wasn't over yet and I had some rounding up of my own to do. For the amount of cattle we were moving, I figured we were going to need about one man for every three hundred head of these mangy beasts we were driving up the trail. I already had one hand from each of the five small ranchers who'd be going along just to make sure I did what I said I would. Not that I blamed them. Me and my boys and these two Juarez lads—if they stuck—would round out the crew to about ten working hands.

"He's the one that was leaning against the bar back there," I said, tossing a thumb over my shoulder toward town, "and kept that barkeep from shotgunning us! That's who he is!" I thought a moment, and decided I'd break it to them right then. "He's also going to be our *cook*."

"You'd let someone as ugly as that cook for us?" It didn't take much to see that Matthew didn't like the idea—or the man.

"Si, señor," Bud started to say, "why he's almost

as . . . nothing, señor, *es nada*." I have never made any claims to being anywhere close to the raving beauty of the Hooker clan. Yes, you can bet I knew what he was going to say. My chin was as full of whiskers and my face just as leathery as Latch Key's, except he wasn't as old as me. Whether he could work the job or not, Bud was looking to stay on the good side of the boss.

"Matthew, you're forgetting your Aunt Sarah," I said as I mounted up. To the Juarez brothers I added, "Woman was uglier than sin, but cooked like everybody's mama."

"I would like to meet this woman some day," Bud said with a smile. Any man who's been on the trail a while can appreciate good cooking.

"Not in your lifetime you won't," I said in a near growl. The thought of her was bringing back bad memories—of her and my sister Callie and her Robert. They'd all died before their time, but then, there were a lot of decent folk who had that day back in '63 when Quantrill burned Lawrence, Kansas, to the ground. It must've showed on my face, for neither my boy or these other two said anything more about Sarah.

"What do you have to find this Latch Key for?" Matthew asked.

"Told me he had some place on the far side of town he was calling home," I said. "After Diah walked into that saloon, I never did get a chance to finish my conversation with him. Gotta find that brother of yours and get some of his money to pay for Latch Key's supplies. Come along if you like."

I wheeled that mount of mine around, heading back toward the central street of town, Mister Henry in one hand, reins in the other. It wasn't long before Matthew pulled up beside me and I noticed the Juarez lads tagging along behind us. We walked those horses through town real easy like, taking notice of the Alamo Saloon where everything had happened. Seemed like every mud hole in Texas had in it an Alamo Saloon. That was another war these folks were still fighting.

Nothing happened there as we passed; I reckon Jared Watts must've put his boys on a leash for a while. Like I said, I had a queasy notion they weren't working the range for him.

It was after we passed the saloon that we heard what sounded like some kind of fracas in the makings at the other end of town. Something in my gut told me we'd better get there right quick. I hadn't seen Diah since the incident at the Alamo Saloon, nor did I know where he'd gone. But there's times you can feel the chill running up your back and you know it isn't warning you about yourself. It's one of your kin it's warning you about. That was the feeling I had now.

"Cold, pa?" Matthew must have seen me shudder.

"No. Let's give these horses a hand getting to that noise up ahead." With that I dug my heels into the side of my mount and felt the presence of Matthew riding right next to me as I pulled up in front of the crowd that was causing all the commotion.

The reason for all the fuss had something to do with Latch Key. They had him seated atop a horse and he didn't look any too comfortable. But then, son, neither would you if you were sitting under the branch of a cottonwood tree, your hands tied behind your back and a rope around your throat. And there, some ten yards off to the side of the horse, was Diah. The street had grown quiet, for it was just him and that Spencer talking to the crowd at the moment.

"I never did like one-sided discussions," Matthew said. He looked as at ease as could be, but I knew that old Sharps he had draped across his arm was ready to do some flame throwing if it came to it, and I'll be damned if it didn't look like it would come to it. Me, I had that Henry of mine in my right hand and just sort of obfusticated the whole bunch of them when I ran my hand inside the big ring I'd had built into the weapon a couple of years back. You see, there was this blacksmith who had a horse stolen from him . . . but that's a whole 'nother canyon. What I had was the crowd's attention, which was good for starters.

"Well, now, folks, this is quite a gathering you got," I said in as pleasant a voice as I could muster. Didn't

want to scare these people like an old mountain man
would've done. No, sir. City folk were *civilized*. And if
you believe that, hoss, *you* can eat my beaver hat!
"Gonna see ary that cottonwood branch is all that strong,
are you? Or maybe see ary that hemp rope is quality
made?"

"Or hold a horse race with no rider?" Matthew threw
in.

"Don't taunt 'em!" Latch Key said in as loud a voice
as he dared, lest his mount get skittish. "Just get me
outta here! And get *her*!"

She had black hair, wore the peasant dress common
to the area, a blouse and skirt, and had a greenish tint to
her eyes that I could see even from where I was sitting.
Not that my own eye sight was all that keen, you understand. It's just that those eyes were about as big as a
frogs at the moment and full of fear. The man standing
behind her didn't seem to be helping any either. He had
one hand wrapped around her waist, holding her to him,
the other big hand covering her mouth. Yup, it was her
eyes that did all the talking now. Believe it, son.

"I would've shot the sonofabitch, but he's standing
too close to her," Diah said in a voice that would've
scared the poison out of a rattler. But we were on the
other side of the crowd and I reckon Matthew thought
he had a better angle on the situation.

"Not for long he ain't." Quicker than an alligator
could chew up a pup, the Sharps was at Matthew's
shoulder. Me, I had to smile some for now the man who
thought he had all of his bets covered had the same sort
of fear in his eyes as the woman he was holding.

"You ain't wanted here, mister," one of the crowd
shouted at us. "You'd better git before we put the both
of you up there on the horse alongside this bastard."
Something in what he said didn't sound right. Hell, he
was talking like there was only me and Matthew and I
knew better than that. Why, we'd come with those two
Juarez lads. Just to be sure, I gave a quick glance over
my shoulder.

They were gone! The horses were there all right, but
they no longer had the riders who'd come with them!

"Damn! Cut'n run," I muttered to myself. Did you
ever feel like you'd put one foot in hell on a dare and the
compadre who was supposed to pull you back out had
decided it was a good time for a walk? Well, if you have,
friend, you know just what was running through my
mind about then.

"Looks like them chilis who come with you done
headed back south of the border," the man said. Real
arrogant, he was. Damn, but I hate those types! Always
acting like they got you by the short hairs.

"Don't call us that." Calm but firm, that's how the
voice sounded. It belonged to Bud. When he stepped
out of the darkness of the alley to our right, he had a
double-barreled shotgun in his hands. And I'll tell you,
son, he didn't look none to friendly either. It's purely
amazing what one word will do to a man.

"Es verdad," came the bass voice of Jorge from the
other side of the street. "Is true" is what it translated to
literally, but "betcherass" is what it meant if the look
on his face and the sound of those two Remingtons
being cocked was any indication. Yes, sir, these Juarez
boys were turning out to be real handy.

"Don't give me none of that, you worthless grea—"
the loudmouth started to say. *Greaser,* that was the
word that was starting to come out of his mouth when
Bud pulled a trigger to that Greener and let a load of
buckshot fly into the ground to one side of this crowd.

The effect was the same as a load of brand new cow
pies dropping flat on top of one of those fancy roulette
wheels. I mean that buckshot was going all over the
place! I even felt a piece whiz past my ear. That shotgun
blast really opened the ball. Yes, sir.

Two shots rang out from a second story window to
my left rear, one of which sent the hat a-flying off the
plug ugly's head; the one who had the woman in front of
him. I couldn't see where the second shot landed. That
first one was enough to make the man go for his gun,
letting loose of the woman's waist. She was just moving

away from him and he was just pulling out his pistol to return fire when that Sharps of Matthew's went off. It spun the man around, knocking the woman to the ground before he fell, too. All of which was just as well for she'd be out of the way. She didn't need to worry any more, for by the time the man was on the ground Diah was standing over him with that Spencer of his. I don't know what it was my son growled to the wounded man, but it stilled him real quick.

The shotgun blast had scared the horse Latch Key was sitting on, but the noose around his neck was no longer attached to the rope that now dangled loosely over the cottonwood. Latch Key's face was as white as a sheet as he rolled off the horse.

I couldn't see who it was who was shooting from that window. Hell, I don't believe anyone else could either. As long as it wasn't me he was shooting at I didn't really care, truth to tell. But it was a whole different story for the flannelmouth who'd been spouting off to me. He and a couple of his friends were about to pepper that open window with a few shots to flush out the shooter up there. That was good enough reason for me to jump in. He was just cocking his handgun when I pulled the reins on my mount some, shifting him to the left enough so that I could kick away the yahoo's pistol before he pulled the trigger. He had the beginnings of a snarl on his face when my Henry rifle cracked him across the back of the skull. Fell to the ground like a Saturday night drunk, he did.

"Smart ass," I spat out. The crowd wasn't a crowd anymore, most of them having scattered to the sides of the street after those shotgun and rifle blasts.

"*Si, señor,*" I heard Bud say, the smile back on his face.

"Got more lip than a muley cow," I said, scowling down at the unconscious man.

"And now a head to match," Bud added. I do believe he was really enjoying this.

Matthew was off his horse now, looking madder than hell. I'd heard him strike one of the others who'd gotten

gun happy, and saw the man fall to the ground. But I
didn't know what it was that had my boy so fired up
until I saw the Sharps lying there on the ground. Trouble
was it wasn't just lying on the dirt there like some other
long gun. The stock was busted off as close as you could
get to the working mechanisms. He must've broken it
when he swung at that yahoo who was now catching
forty winks on the ground. Mad? Shoot, you fool with
one of Matthew's guns and he'd charge hell with a
bucket of water, put out the fire, then skate on the ice
until he found out what pile of coal you were hiding
behind.

Matthew charged what was left of the hanging party.
He hit one with a left and then a right, then did it to
another of the group. Those whom Matthew wasn't thinning out right quick were leaving on a voluntary basis.
Didn't have a desire to take a nap this time of the day I
reckon.

It couldn't have taken more than a minute or two, as
big as he is, until he was standing there all alone. Sweaty,
hatless, and still looking mean. It was when he was
reaching down for his hat that I saw one of the sideline
crowd pull a gun and step out into the street. If it wasn't
for the fact that he held it so steady I might had missed
when I shot the gun out of his hand. That Henry .44 slug
must have busted up his hand if not his gun, for he gave
out a brief cry of agony before grabbing the hand with
his other one.

I walked my horse up to him, gave him as mean a look
as he was giving me, twirled that Henry around on the
ring lever and pointed it right at his chest.

"I'll get you for this, you—"

"Hooker's the name, sonny. Black Jack Hooker. You
try getting me and I'll guarantee you that ary you do, my
reflexes will take you with me. Now," I said, pushing
him back with the barrel of the Henry, "you pull a
weapon on my boys again in your lifetime"—I grinned—
"well, you won't have much of a lifetime."

I walked the mount over to where Diah was still

standing guard over the cur who'd used a woman as a shield.

"I'll put you in jail for this!" the wounded man said to Matthew.

"Sure thing, Guns," Diah said to his brother. "Ain't that a kicker?" Slowly, the barrel of his Spencer pulled back the vest the man wore, revealing a deputy marshal's badge. There was a moment of silence before he spoke again. "Thanks, Guns. I appreciate it."

"Anything for a brother, Diah." I had a notion that any feuding between the two had come to a halt—at least temporarily.

"Who are you?" I said to the woman, "and what is it I'm getting in all this trouble for?"

"My name is Maria." She had a husky voice, the kind you figure on hearing from a saloon woman.

"Latch Key and this deputy were going to war over her when I got here," Diah said by way of explanation. "Our fearless lawman was calling her a whore and Latch Key lit into him. Drew a crowd and pretty soon the deputy had some of the town drunks convinced that he'd been attacked by Latch Key and that Latch Key oughtta be strung up. That's pretty much how it was until they got him on the horse. Maria was about ready to scream for help so the deputy grabbed hold of her and told her to shut up, then ordered the rest of the crowd to hang him." Diah nodded toward Latch Key. "I told 'em all to stop it, and we had us a Mexican stand off until you rode up."

I gave the woman a hard look out of the corner of my eye.

"That true? You one of the ladies of—"

"She's my wife!" Latch Key blurted out. I couldn't tell whether that was something these folks didn't know or what, but you can bet it had a definite effect on my view of my new cook. That hard look of mine was now focused on the scruffy little man before me, and you bet he could read in it that I wasn't all that keen about what I'd just learned. Why, I would've put him back up on that horse and hung him my own self!

"Do tell," were the only words that accompanied my stare.

Chapter 4

Nobody said much of anything until we got back to that cottonwood, not even the folks on the streets. Especially not the folks on the streets. Oh, the women who passed us gave those hellacious looks to Maria that said they knew what she *really* was, but I had a notion she didn't care any more than I did. Hell, if looks could kill, I'd have been dead before I reached manhood.

"Handy with them guns, boys," I said, dismounting.

"*Si.*" Bud was still remembering it, still grinning at the fun he'd had. Jorge, he didn't say much of anything.

"For a minute there I almost thought—"

"*Si, señor,*" Bud replied with a knowing look. "I know. I know." Things like the Alamo and that Mexican War had a good many folks hereabout doubting the abilities of these· south of the border fellows. If you listened to the stories, you'd find out they weren't worth spit when it came to fighting with short and long guns, and I could understand that because the Mexicans . . . well, they'd had the damndest luck with pistols and rifles when it came to war time. What seldom got mentioned was that if you put one of them around anything that had an edge to it, why, they could carve you open something fierce. Shoot, boy, I could tell you stories . . .

"You fixing to stay awhile?" I asked Matthew, who had yet to dismount. He still had that madder than hell look about him, the one that warned everyone not to tangle with him. Not that I could blame him. Hell, all he had for a weapon now was a long barreled rifle with no stock to it at all. Useless as buffalo chips on your plate instead of in your fire, that's what it was.

"Actually, I was thinking of going back and seeing if that big time lawman wanted to take a crack at putting me away," he said. Ain't no one else but his mother ever got hold of that boy to straighten him out in his youth. Me, I was gone a lot so she had her hands full, Martha did. Powerful woman, that one. Only woman for me as far as I was ever concerned. Now I had to find a way around having a knock-down-drag-out fight with the boy to keep him from going off and getting himself killed. Confrontations like these were the ones that made me remember that he missed his mother as much as I did.

"Martha told me for the longest time that she brung you up right, son. I believed her. I'd hate to think—"

"Don't do it, Pa," was his short fused reply. I had him where he didn't want to be and he knew it. He was full of hatred at having that Sharps busted up and the thought of getting some revenge. All of a sudden I'd dropped his mother into the conversation and had his conscience fighting with his feelings. It ain't always easy being a father.

"That was very brave, what you did back there," Maria said in that husky voice of hers. She must've figured out who we were talking about and decided to get in on the conversation. Well, hoss, I *undecided* her right quick.

"Shut up!" Not a snarl, you understand, just two words that were said in one hellacious mean manner. It worked, too. Could've backhanded her across the face, she looked that shocked.

"Wait a minute," Latch Key said, growing a frown of his own, "you can't talk to her that way." He was taking a step closer to me as he said it, steam trailing out of him by the time he finished spouting off. That was mostly because the business end of Mister Henry was stuck under his belt. Does it every time.

"Well, I just did, friend, so you're a bit late." I'll tell you, son, I'd about had it with people just running off at the mouth like they were the Ohio River joining the Mississippi. Damn but I hate pushy people. "Best thing you could do right now would be to see can you actually live up to your brag. I always need coffee, Latch Key, so see if you can boil us some."

"But—"

"Diah, show him what provisions you've got and get a list of what you're going to need."

"Right, Pa." At least one of my sons was listening to me.

"There must be something you and old Frog Throat can be doing around here," I said to Bud. I had a notion his brother didn't care for what I'd called him, but all I got was a soft-spoken *"Si"* and they were gone.

"You get off'n that horse," I said, cocking an eye at Matthew, "and you," I added, turning to Maria, "plant yourself right there. If I don't get the answers I want, by God, I'll uproot you quicker'n lightning through a gooseberry bush!"

Like I said, I don't like pushy people and it was amazing how quickly the whole crowd quieted down. Why, Matthew was getting off his horse and the woman, well, she'd either gotten cold or scared the way she was shivering.

"Way I figure it, son, we're gonna have more'n enough trouble to suit us on this drive coming up. I ain't got no use to go looking for any more than we've run into so far today.

"As for your long gun, well, don't feel all alone about it," I said, bringing up Mister Henry and turning it so he could see the huge dent in the receiver underneath the barrel. It didn't take more than one gander to see that I wouldn't be able to fire the usual fifteen shots anymore. That was the one fault the Henry rifle had, but I'd been willing to put up with it in exchange for the firepower I'd gotten from it.

"How'd that happen?" The mad seemed to be gone from Matthew's tone now, replaced by concern for my rifle.

"Got so mad back there that I forgot about not using the barrel to whack that fella up 'longside the head. Come at him full from the right and hit him with the receiver and barrel. Couldn't fire more'n two or three out of this now. So you ain't the only one ailing for a decent firearm."

He's the tallest of all us Hookers, Matthew is, but he had a humble look about him now. I didn't know if it was because he'd been going up against me, his father, or was remembering what I'd said about his mother, or feeling sad about Mister Henry. Take your pick. Me, I didn't care as long as I succeeded in calming him down some.

"I see," he said in a calm voice.

"Don't fret, boy." I smiled. "I got us some new ones cached for the start of the drive." That put the light back in his eyes, just like it was Christmas Eve. Guns were the toys this lad played with. Hell, that's how he got his nickname! "Once we get settled in, I'll show 'em to you," I said.

"Good enough." He grinned and then he was gone. That left me and Maria, who was still acting like she had a chill.

"Sister, I don't know what saloon you come out of and I don't really care." My frown was back again and she knew I meant business. "What I do know is you're trouble. Got so I can spot it right off in a woman, that's a fact."

She shrugged, moving her shoulder the way you'd expect a loose woman like her to do. Most men, I reckon they'd be looking for part of her blouse to fall off that shoulder, but like I say, since Martha had died there hadn't been anyone for me. Never would be.

"Maybe I'll change your luck," she said in a sultry voice.

"Right. And I'm Moses. Look," I said, jabbing a finger at the air before her, "I don't want you along on this drive, so you just say your good-byes to Latch Key and go back to wherever—"

I never did finish what I was saying. Hearing a pistol or rifle going off in this land usually does that to a body, if you know what I mean. As long as you can hear them you know that they ain't shooting at you—or haven't hit you at least. But this explosion was right around the corner and it sounded like a muffled version of Diah's Spencer.

If it had been a race to see who got there first, I do believe they'd judge it a tie, for Maria and I rounded that corner side by side. I gave a short sigh of relief when I saw that Diah was still standing, but Maria ran quickly to Latch Key's side, looking at the bloodied side of his leg.

"Oh, my God!" she said, apparently not all that used to blood or the sight of it.

"What the hell—" Matthew said, arriving with the Juarez lads behind him.

"That's what I'd like to know," I added.

"They said it could happen, but I never figured it would," Diah said, suddenly sporting one of those looks that said he was guilty as hell about something.

"Happened? What? What happened?" I sputtered.

"Will one of you men help me get—" Maria was saying, but the Juarez boys had read her mind, for Bud was easing Latch Key down to the ground so he could lean against a wagon wheel, while Jorge climbed into the wagon to ferret out some medicinals.

"I heard it too, Pa," Matthew said. "Those Spencers have a rep for sometimes having cartridges explode in the magazine if they get jarred around too much."

"He's right," Diah confirmed. "I reckon Latch Key set my rifle down a mite too hard."

"Whatever he done, it ain't a rifle any more," his brother said.

Looking down at the shattered stock of the Spencer laying beside the wounded man, I could see he was right. Latch Key must have set the butt of the rifle down with more force than usual. It would account for the broken stock and grotesque shape of what was once the firing mechanism of the rifle. The color was starting to come back to Latch Key's face now, making me think he likely had some stray pieces of metal in that leg rather than a bullet.

"Helluva fix," I muttered. Not that I was unconcerned about Latch Key himself, you understand. It's just that I was thinking I'd gained and lost a cook all in one day. "How in the hell am I gonna find another cook on this short a notice?" I was talking more to myself than anyone.

"Don't you go counting me out," Latch Key said, gamey as ever. "I might have a bad leg, but these hands is what're going to cook your meals."

"That's right," Maria added, sounding a bit defiant her own self. "I can help him with whatever he needs. If necessary I'll do the cooking, too." That was feisty for as scared as she'd been a few minutes back.

"Not if I have anything to say about it." That's what I was figuring on saying, but the hard, harshly spoken words didn't come from me.

Over my shoulder I saw my trail boss, Tom Lang, and his crew of five, most of them looking like they'd back his words to the hilt.

Chapter 5

Like I said, I'd gotten awful tired of pushy people that day. Tom Lang, well, he wasn't exactly known for pulling his horns in when he ought to. If what I had heard was true, he was as feisty as either of my boys and maybe even a mite tougher to boot. That speaks well of a man . . . unless, of course, he's the one that got the rumor going in the first place. All of which made no difference to me. The way I was feeling, why, I figured I'd pull his horns off or punch them in, one.

"What you got a say in here, son, don't concern nothing more'n getting them longhorns of yours to market in one piece," I said, squinting as I slowly turned to face him. "I'll say who goes and who don't and when." I threw in a mite more crust to both the squint of my eye and the tone of my voice when I added, "I damn sure hope you can run them four-leggeds as good as you do that mouth of yours, Lang. You don't and I'm gonna make sure that *you* don't make it to trail's end, leastwise not with us."

The look he gave he would've curdled the morning milk if I'd been a cow.

"Look, I know what she is," he all but growled.

"So do I." I gave a leery glance at Maria, wondering if I wasn't letting myself in for more trouble than I already knew I'd have on this drive. "She's going along as my cook's assistant.'' That brought smiles of satisfaction from both Latch Key and Maria. "And that, son, is that.''

"Listen, you old—''

"That's a mistake, Tom.'' Matthew had stepped in, although I didn't know why. "Last time I called him old, he beat me four ways from Sunday.'' If there'd been such a time I didn't remember it, not of late anyways. On the other hand, at the moment I didn't really care, especially since it put a halt to Tom Lang's complaining. He was somewhere between my oldest and youngest boy in build and I'd fought men his size before. It's just that the day wasn't even over yet and I felt like I'd had my fill of fighting for at least the week, if not the month. And Tom Lang, well, when he got mean and went on the prod, I had a hunch it was going to be an ugly kind of mean. Like I said, I'd had my fill.

"Who's watching the herd?'' I asked after what seemed one hell of a long piece of silence.

"Slim.''

"Good man. I'll talk to him later. Right now I've got a job for you fellas.'' Lang wasn't too keen on being told what to do, but I had him unload a couple of heavy boxes from the wagon, and he and his men did it. It was then that I pulled Maria off to the side to talk with her alone.

"Now, you listen to me, sister. I said you were trouble. That fella back there was about to call you a whore. Same thing is going to apply to you as does to Tom Lang or anyone else. You carry your load or leave. Understand?'' I still didn't sound too friendly in the way I said it.

"Think you can handle trouble?'' she asked in a voice that sounded curious more than anything. "Latch Key was telling me it was bad luck to have a woman on a drive.''

"Yeah, there's that. Me, I been in trouble since whoever flung the first chunk. And as for luck . . . well, lady, you make your own luck. Just stay in line and stay out of the way.''

No confirmation. Nothing verbal. Just a sweet smile. I'd come to distrust those kinds of smiles from women like Maria. You could read too much into them and you damn well never knew what was really behind them.

"All right, Hooker," Lang growled when I returned, "you've got the boxes. Now we got to get back to work."

"Find a place for your git up end first, boys. I got to edicate you about something." Most of them simply squatted down the way they did before a fire. "Matthew, see can you open that lid." I was smiling all the while, knowing that Lang wouldn't like it one bit. "Seems Lang has got him some reservations about me and my boys. Maybe the rest of you do, too. Ary that's the case, I'm here to tell you I've taken out some extry protection." Before I could say any more, I heard the sound of a nail being pulled from the box top to my rear.

"What is it, Guns?" Diah was suddenly moving toward him, although I'd gauge he likely knew what it was his brother was looking at. Matthew "Guns" Hooker had that ogle-eyed look every youngster has on Christmas morning. What he brought out of that box was a new toy for him to play with, one that would probably save his life. He tossed one to me before picking out another to examine more closely.

"A Henry, right?" Shorty asked.

"Not quite," I said. "Some are calling it the Improved Henry and I'll tell you, son, if that's what they want to call it that's fine with me. Fella by the name of Winchester bought up the company making the Henry, but Winchester or Henry—don't make no never mind to me—it damn sure is *improved!*"

"Where'd you get 'em, Pa?" Diah asked.

"When it seemed like we had us a chance of putting together one of these trail drive fandangos, I took me a trip back east to see could I get some more Henrys. Gotta have a good long gun on a drive like this." I smiled, then shook my head in silence.

"Well, what happened, Pa?"

"Don't never go back east, son. Never! Most uppity

bunch of humans I ever did see. Got a disposition worse'n them longhorns out there. Worse than Tom Lang, if that's possible!'' A couple of the men laughed until Lang threw them a glare. "Only good thing come out of it was these rifles.''

I then spent a few minutes telling these young bucks just what it was about this Improved Henry that was going to make a life and death difference for them on the trail. Had their attention all the while, too. You start to palavering about one more way you can stay alive to tell about it in this land, why, you can guarantee a man's full attention, son.

Except for the changes in it, the weapon was designed after the Henry rifle, which is why Shorty mistook it at first. Oh, it still fired the same .44 caliber Flat Rim Fire cartridge Mister Henry did. And the guts of the mechanism and lever action were still the same. But there were three significant changes that made this rifle worthy of being called "Improved."

The first was the method of loading. On the Henry you had to load the magazine from the barrel end of the rifle. Oh, you could load and fire a good thirty rounds a minute if you were good at it, but you had to have enough room to allow you to load properly and that wasn't always possible. If you got pinned down behind a log you'd likely get your top knot taken from you while you were trying to reload. This new rifle had changed all that. The right side of the frame now had what they called a spring-closed loading port directly to the rear of the tubular magazine. It was a hell of a lot easier—and faster—to load those .44s now. Just like the Henry, it took fifteen rounds, although you could push seventeen in if you tried hard.

The second was the magazine tube itself. Mister Henry's magazine was slotted, which made it easy for all sorts of dirt, dust, or any other foreign matter to get in amongst your ammunition and block up the system when you needed it working the most. It also made the magazine weak and easy to bend, as I had experienced earlier in the day. This new model I held in my hand now had one entire tube for its magazine. It was much sturdier and, along with the new loading port, eliminated the possibility of getting dirt and such in the magazine.

The third improvement was one that would seem minor only to those who just look at a rifle but never have reason to use it daily like I do. These so-called civilized townfolks go out every so often to do some hunting and leave their rifle setting in the corner of the room or over a mantel the rest of the time. Me, son, I've been in more than one scrape that called for one hell of a lot of firepower—and HOW! Fought with Carson at Adobe Walls in '64 and chased up some Confederate raiders the year before that. Mister Henry, he saved my life more than once. What this new model had was a wooden forearm, something my Henry didn't have.

"So what?" Lang said, still not impressed.

"Pilgrim," I muttered in disgust, shaking my head.

"What did you say?" Lang was looking like he was about to get mean. His men seemed to be taking offense as well. Now, son, no man worth his salt likes being called a pilgrim, especially if he's been around a while in this land.

"You lying—" Lang started to say as he and his crew commenced to get up off their haunches. The others made it to their feet, but Tom Lang took a stiff arm in the chest that knocked him off balance and flat onto the shiny part of his pants.

I didn't have to worry about the others, for those Juarez boys stepped up alongside one each while my boys did the same. Not a word spoken, you understand. It was all instinct. In fact, I'd say about the only sound made was those bones of mine creaking the way they do as I squatted down to Lang's level.

"Don't ever call a man a liar just because he knows more'n you do, son." It came out like it had taken a trip across a field of gravel, but there was no mistaking the words or their seriousness. Lang, he didn't like it one bit. Me, I just squatted there and eyeballed him while I read to him from the book.

"Me and Carson took on 'bout half the Injuns in the

world back in '64 up by Abode Walls. One point in that shootout, I fired upwards of a hundred rounds without stopping for so much as to catch my breath and reload, Lang. Too busy shooting at the Comanch' to notice much else 'til it was over with. That's when I noticed *this*."

I held up the paw I call a left hand, watched his eyes grow some as he inspected it. What he saw was a thick, ugly scar on the outside of my thumb where there used to be skin. The ends of all four fingers and half of the last knuckle on each were just as ugly, with a cross between a thick callous and a permanent scar.

"Time ever comes you get you into a good shooting match with one of these rifles, Lang, you feel that barrel when you get through. Damn things get plenty hot ary you pour 'nough lead through 'em. Hot 'nough to take the very skin off your fingers. If you get my drift. That's why I'm partial to that wood forearm."

I stood up then, those same bones creaking again. Every time I heard them I had to wonder if I'd make it as a scout sneaking through the Indian country. Hell, you could hear the damn things for a mile off! But that was the least of my problems at the moment. Tom Lang had been bested and didn't like it. The look in his eyes said so and he was doing some serious thinking about righting the situation with his own kind of justice.

"Still got that brass frame, I see," Latch Key said after what seemed a long pause.

"Yup. Just as brassy as my boys." I smiled at him, giving Lang as much chance as he'd get to call off the fight. Mean as he could be, he was still a damn good hand with those longhorns.

"Sounds like the perfect weapon," Lang said, although the way he was looking at me I had to wonder if they weren't just words to fill the air.

"For the most part. Only one thing I'm disappointed in," I said.

"What's that?"

"Can't really tell who made the thing, should you get a need to send for a few extrys to have on hand."

"He's right," Matthew said. Out of the corner of my eye I could see him looking over the weapon from barrel to butt, coming to the realization that there was indeed no brand on this new stray calf.

"From what I could find out, this shirtmaker named Winchester now owns the company they come from. Ary these things are as good as they claim, why, shoot, the man oughtta put his name on 'em," I said.

"Sounds right," Shorty said. "Old Sam Colt sure made it plain that what you had in your fist was one of his. What did you say they were calling this rifle?"

"Improved Henry, Winchester, hell, I don't know," I shrugged. "Take your pick. All I wanted you boys to know was that I got one of these for every man in the crew." That seemed to lighten the spirits of all but Tom Lang.

"Expecting trouble?" he asked.

"Sonny, I always expect trouble. Hell, I just had a run in with you, didn't I?"

"Yeah, you did at that," he replied, rubbing his chin. It was likely as close as he'd come that day to getting any grudging respect from me. Now all he had to do was figure out if I was just saying it to keep him on as a working hand, or if I really meant it.

Let him stew, I figured.

Chapter 6

Latch Key lived up to his brag. The next morning he got up with me, maybe a mite earlier, for that fire was already going and the black scalded coffee pot on top of it. Best thing a body could wake up to was coffee on the brew, Martha used to say. I do believe that's the only thing I ever argued about with that woman. You see, son, I always favored waking up next to Martha. Hell, how do you think those two boys of mine come about?!

"Not bad, Latch Key," I said, tasting the first cup of the hot stuff a few minutes later. I reckon he was as ill tempered as any other man first thing in the morning. His only response was a grumble as he set about making the morning meal.

Me, I wasn't going to get on his bad side, not this early in the morning. Maria was up, too, so I simply faded back into the shadows to watch the man I'd hired to feed this crew. It was still dark and the only light I could see by was the fire, but I had a curious feeling about those two. They just didn't fit. A crotchety fellow like Latch Key—God only knew what his real name was—and a looker like Maria who was anything but Mexican. Oh, he'd tell her to do this and that and she would, moving right quick when she did. But just like I figured, she was going to be trouble.

Part of it was the fact that she *was* a good-looking

37

woman. I'll tell you, hoss, I think I'd rather have the homeliest woman who ever lived on this drive with me than Maria. All she had to wear was a man's work shirt and some denims that were getting to be the work uniform of the range. Didn't matter whether you were a brush popper, a bronc buster, or even a farmer, denims were what you wore to get the job done. Of course, they were also made of the only material sturdy enough to do outdoors work in west of the Mississippi. Now, the pair Maria was wearing wasn't all that tight, but I knew that all it would take was a good washing in the creek to form fit those pants to her. Hell, same thing happens with my buckskins.

It wasn't the denims that bothered me so much as the way she tucked that work shirt into them. Lordy! I don't know about all that rigging a woman has to deal with when she puts on her pretties, son, but Maria didn't have any of those problems. When I say she moved quick, well, it wasn't just her get up end that did the moving! And, son, if you need more explanation than that, I sure do hope you enjoy living with those Franciscan monks.

I was approaching the tailgate of the chuck wagon about the same time as she was walking away. Latch Key, he wasn't paying much attention to her. Not that I wanted him to, you understand. Hell, that was something I didn't need, a cook who was too distracted to do his cooking.

"Think you got enough food made to give these lads a start?" I asked. "We're burning daylight." The sun hadn't even begun to come near the eastern horizon, but I knew full well that moving these longhorns was going to be about the same as trapping those beaver way back when. You work from "can see" to "can't see" and get as much done as you can.

"Yeah," Latch Key grumbled, not even looking up from his work. "I just sent Maria to get Lang and his men up." He stopped then, stock still, the way you do when something hits you. As he glanced up at me, there was a frown on his face with just a touch of curiosity to it. "I been meaning to ask you, just how come you waited this long to get you a cook? Hell, roundup's near over in a day or so." The distrust in his voice now showed on his face. "I do believe I'd like to know why."

I didn't have a chance to answer the question. Behind me there was a shrill scream, the kind that only a woman can give. I dropped my coffee cup as I spun around, ready to pour lead into whoever or whatever was hurting her. But I wasn't the only one. Every one of Lang's men, Bud and his brother, and my own two boys had a pistol or rifle trained in the general direction of Maria. As for Maria, well, hoss, I could only see her get up end, leaning over like she was, but I suspicioned that the look on her face was the same as that I'd seen the day before. She was leaning over Tom Lang, who had hold of her arm, keeping her in place while his other hand held a pistol shoved into her chest.

"You trying to get yourself killed, lady?" It didn't come out as his usual growl but rather an even uglier, meaner string of words, and that's saying something with a man like Lang.

"I was just trying to wake you up," she said in a whisper that could be heard all over camp.

"Well, you do it again and you're—"

"—gonna be just as dead as you will be after you plug her, Lang," I said, jacking a round into the chamber of my rifle. If you've got to be told that I had that Winchester pointed at Lang, well, son, you haven't been paying attention.

"Put it away, Lang," Latch Kay said. "I'm the only one gets to tickle my wife. You don't take that six-gun of yours outta her ribs, I'll make you eat it for breakfast."

It was damndest thing you ever did see. Latch Key, he'd seen the whole thing happen from the start, but when I glanced over my shoulder as he spoke, why, he wasn't even looking at Tom Lang. Said his piece and kept on cutting away with that cleaver of his like nothing was happening. Of course, there were a couple of words he said that got some extra emphasis from that cleaver coming down just a mite harder than usual. Otherwise he just kept on doing his job.

I don't know if it was the words or the sound of that cutting tool that made Lang take the gun out of her ribs, but he did just that. Maria left him quick, and I knew that by the time she got back to the chuck wagon all that shaking she was doing had nothing at all to do with the chill in the morning air. Not hardly.

The rest of them put away their guns, too, silently rolling their bed rolls and tossing them in the back of the wagon. The next stop was that coffee pot and its contents. Like I said, Latch Key lived up to his brag because no one complained about the food. Not that I expected them to after what had happened. Besides, the grub was pretty good. The hard part was sitting through a meal with all that silence, each of us waiting to see who would be the first to talk. It was Lang himself who broke the silence.

"Gonna finish up our end today, Hooker," he said as though nothing had happened. "You gonna be able to find a wrangler for that remuda by tomorrow?"

"Ary I don't, I've got a couple of volunteers who'll be glad to pitch in." I tossed a glance and a devilish smile at Diah and Matthew. They were as surprised as Lang and the rest.

"Guns?! Why he's so damn big that—" Tom Lang, he wasn't having any success this morning when it came to completing a full sentence.

"Tell me something, Lang," Matthew interrupted, sopping a biscuit in some grease. He could be fiery, this boy, but he surprised me with the softness of his voice now. Calm, real calm. That was what worried me. "You like beef steak, do you?"

"Yeah, sure. Why?" Lang was a mite puzzled now.

"Oh, nothing," Matthew said, polishing off the biscuit in one bite, washing it down with half a cup of coffee as he stood up. Lang came to his feet, too, but he was still about three or four inches shy of Matthew's height. Lang was big all right, but Matthew, he just *was*. "It's just that it's hard to chew anything that good when you ain't got no teeth." Matthew smiled, looking just as devilish as I had.

No disputing it, Tom Lang didn't like those words. He also had a habit of letting his pistol do his talking for him. He was going for it when Matthew dropped his coffee cup. By the time the cup hit the ground, my boy had his hand fast around Lang's wrist, digging his thick fingers into it until the trail boss released his grip on the weapon.

"It's also hard to pick your teeth up off the ground when you've got a couple of busted hands." With grit teeth, the look of death, and a voice right out of the north side of hell, that's how Matthew said his piece this time. Got Lang's attention, too, he did.

"Better let him go, son. We got better things to do than play dare around here," I said. Matthew released his grip, but the anger didn't leave Lang's eyes as he rubbed his wrist. Can't say as I blamed him either.

"That's right," Diah added, speaking up for the first time this morning. "Like finding us a wrangler." He was looking right at me when he said it and it wasn't any too friendly a look either.

I think he was trying to tell me he didn't like the idea of being a wrangler at all.

Chapter 7

If you're wondering why my boys got a bit uppity at being volunteered to be wranglers, well, they had good reason. During the roundup I'd heard nothing but complaints or jokes about wranglers. Fact is, they weren't held in too high an esteem by any of the men who went out and did the brush popping and branding—what they considered the real work a hand should be doing.

"What's the matter?" I asked Bud Juarez as Lang and his men headed out to the herds. There was just enough light coming over the horizon to give me a clear look at the small Mexican shaking his head.

"It is a shame, *amigo,* how you people bastardize my language," he said, still shaking his head in what looked to be disbelief.

"Run that by me again, son. I didn't get the winner of that horse race." The boy was purely obfusticating.

"You take my *caverango* and make it "wrangler"; my *juzgado* becomes your "hoosegow." He shrugged. "It is a shame."

"I see. Well, son, ary you want to discuss politics, it'll have to wait until we can't see. Right now we gotta find us a wrangler." I wasn't waiting for any more discussion, and had turned on my heel to go get my horse, but stopped when I heard Matthew chuckle. When he caught up with me, I asked him what it was all about.

"Nothing, Pa," he said, letting out a chuckle again. "When Bud asked me how politics had got into the conversation, I just told him that whenever you heard the word *bastard,* you figured the conversation had to do with politicians, most of 'em being bastards at best."

He was right, too. Most of those fellows were looking out for their own interests more than anyone else's. Hell, I was surprised they allowed as many as they did on this side of the Mississippi!

Bud Juarez though, he had a point. When you start working your way into what was once another man's land, why, you pick up some of his lingo, some of his ways. You'd never hear a Texican admit to it, but he learned quite a bit about cattle and ranching from the *vaquero,* the Mexican version—or Spanish, if you like—of the men who were now working the cattle in Texas.

"You gonna be all right, Latch Key?" I asked, stopping by the chuck wagon once the Juarez mounts and my own were saddled up. Me, I was talking to Latch Key, but the rest of them were giving Maria a look or two. Hell, they were staring is what they were doing!

"I'll get by," he said. "Wound ain't as bad as I figured it would be. You could do something for me. You see Lang and his crew, tell 'em to bring in some firewood if they want to eat another hot meal or have coffee." He gave a hard look to the rest of the riders before him. "You boys don't put your eyeballs back in their sockets, why, you won't find no deadwood either."

"Maria, you pull that shirt out of them britches." My comment drew surprised glances from everyone, including Maria.

"What the hell—" You never heard five men and a woman say the same thing at the same time in more perfect unison.

"Do it," I growled, just in case one of them had an urge for a fight.

Maria did it. Slow enough so all of us got a handy glimpse of skin as she did, her glaring at me all the while. When the shirt was out, it draped loosely over the top of her waist and down some. Oh, she was still there, if you know what I mean. It's just that it wasn't all that noticeable anymore . . . which ain't saying much.

"How am I supposed to work like this?" she asked defiantly, eyes still blazing. No, sir, she didn't like it one bit.

"Why, darlin', now you got you a breeze maker to keep you cooled off," I said, giving her a mischievous smile. "Keep that shirt tucked in like you had it, why, the snow on top of them mountains woulda melted by high noon. Honest."

The blaze in those eyes had turned to thunder and lightning, hoss, and I had no intention of waiting around for it to strike! As I recall, Latch Key was trying to keep her from taking his butcher knife away from him while the rest us got the hell out of there. You can bet that when we came back for coffee, we'd be sitting back to back if she hadn't cooled off. Maybe even if she had.

I saw him on the horizon. He looked black from that distance, but then, most men were tanned pretty dark out here. His partner was sitting tight in the saddle; that or he was skinnier than those telegraph poles they'd been putting up. Whichever, they had my attention as we rode up to them. It was when they became more visible that I saw the first man actually was a black man. The reason the fellow riding with him was sitting pole straight was because the black man had a rope hitched full to his middle, keeping his arms at his sides. Maybe that was why the second man had a meaner-than-hell look on his face.

"I do believe I have something you want, Mister Hooker," the black man said. He was pleasant enough about it, acting almost too sure of himself, considering the fact that he could have been shot out of the saddle by any one of us. There was still a lot of talk about what a Negro was worth, even with the war over and all, so seeing this one acting the way he was put me in a mind to be cautious. He was either a hell of a bluffer or he had guts, one. Turned out it was a bit of both.

"Well, now, ain't too often these days I get something

given to me," I said, cocking a suspicious eye at him. "Would your present be your friend here . . . or the rider out to my right?"

"You're very good, Mister Hooker." He smiled, and raised the Henry rifle he gripped in his left hand high into the air so his compadre riding through the trees could see it. I knew my boys and the Juarezs would be taking in the new hand being dealt this game, so I kept my own eyes on the man before me.

"Gotta be to get this . . . experienced." I wasn't about to mention the word *old*, even if I did feel like it some days. "There's three of us here that answer to the monicker Hooker, son," I said as his partner walked his horse toward us. "That makes me curious. Gets me to wondering how it is you know my name and who it is told it to you."

"Why, I'm addressing you, Black Jack." Still smiling, he was, but acting a whole lot more educated than most folks would picture a black man being. "As for how I know your name"—here he shrugged, noncommittally—*"quien sabe?"*

"Who knows? Wish I did."

"All in due time."

His compadre turned out to be an Indian. He was as buckskinned and tan as me, except he'd never had a need to step out in the sun to get that deep a tan. No chin whiskers, of course, but the hair was black, as were the eyes, the cheekbones high. Sitting there, he had that dull, complacent look an Indian will give you on first meeting. But it was a front that said you could bank on him being just as dangerous as he didn't appear. He, too, carried a long gun.

"My partner, Eagle Feather," the black rider said by way of introduction.

"How," came the deep voice of the redman.

"Beats the hell outta me." This was getting to be some group I was gathering. "By the by, son," I added, turning back to the black man, "since we're tossing names around here, just what is it I should call you?"

"John is fine." He shrugged again. "Long John if you

like." That last would fit him all right, for the man was as long of leg as he was muscular above the waist. A rangy sort, you might say.

"Then just who is this bird?" I said, looking at the poor specimen of a man in the saddle next to him. The prisoner hadn't said anything because there was a bandana of sorts stuck into his mouth. The trickle of blood coming out the side of his mouth was enough indication that, meaner-than-hell or not, this yahoo had come out second best in a two-man fight. "Might talk better ary you took that bandana outta his mouth."

"As you wish." Long John's smile was leaving right quick, replaced by a look of disappointment.

With a quickness that was surprising for a man his size, he shifted his left hand from the barrel of the Henry back to the lever and trigger, the rifle seemingly suspended in midair. With his right hand he grabbed an edge of the bandana and jerked it from the man's mouth. The part that had been inside his mouth was covered with blood, but not nearly as much as he then spit out twice, deliberately using Long John's long legs as his target.

"Well, don't just sit there! Get me loose!" he half mumbled through the empty spaces where some teeth used to be. Without waiting for an answer, he gave a hateful glare at the two men who, apparently, held him captive. "A redskin and a goddamn— "

Everyone knew what he was going to say, especially Long John. So that rifle of his coming down across the man's nose was no surprise. It must've been the mad that kept this bloodied man going, for he was mumbling and screaming at the same time. Long John stuffed that bandana back in the man's mouth, but it didn't do a hell of a lot of good for all the blood coming down out the man's nose. Diah lifted a leg over the rear of his horse, as though to dismount, but stopped halfway when the black man spoke.

"Don't touch him."

For an ex-slave he was making every use of free speech he could, adding a dash of cold harshness to the words he spoke. Business, that's what he was talking. This lad was conducting. Seeing Eagle Feather sitting on his mount slowly shaking his head back and forth wasn't an encouraging sign for the man who was thinking of going up against these two. No, sir.

"He is bleeding bad, *mi amigo*," Bud said.

"Friend, I don't care if he bleeds to death," Long John answered. You might say the conversation sort of dried up about then, although Diah had a concerned look about him. I reckon he always did have more compassion than his brother or me. Long John, he must've seen that in the boy's face, for it was Diah he spoke to now. "You won't care if he dies either, after I get through telling you what he near done." Then he turned his attention back to me. "I understand you like to palaver, Mister Hooker. Why don't we take a ride while I tell you about this man."

"Got a direction your stick's a-floating?"

"As a matter of fact, I do, sir. Right over there," he said, pointing in the general direction of Jared Watts' spread.

Long John was right. By the time we got to Watts' outfit, there wasn't none of us who cared whether the man he had tied up lived or died. Fact is I had a real urge to kill him right then and there. Only thing I wanted worse was to kill Jared Watts.

"Where's your boss?" I growled at some hands when we reached Watts' so-called ranch. I couldn't see anything on it that looked like it didn't need repair of some sort. The only sounds to be heard were those of some brute in a far side corral who had taken a bullwhip to a mustang, likely figuring he was gonna tame him with it. Ranch, my ass!

"Mister Watts ain't available," one gunman said, planting both hands on his hips as if he were some sort of oak tree that defied being cut down.

"Then make him available!" They were Diah's words and they were damn businesslike. The bloodied yahoo had passed out halfway to the Watts place, the only thing keeping him in his saddle being Diah, who'd held

onto his arm the rest of the way. You could tell he
wasn't too awful concerned about the man's health anymore when he let go the arm, giving it a shove to make
sure the yahoo fall off his mount. While everyone took
in that action, I slid off my own horse, rifle in hand, and
took a step toward the loudmouth.

"Joe?" one of the men said. Squinting the way he did,
it seemed he was having trouble making out the man's
features.

"Shut up, Phil," the oak tree said, suddenly concerned about what his compadre was saying. To me, he
added, "You'd have to go through me to see the boss,
old man, and grizzled as you are, why, I don't think you
can." He smiled confidently, giving a glance to either
side of him, bragging to his cronies, "See, boys, got the
old bastard shaking in his boots already."

Shaking? You bet I was! But it had nothing to do with
this flannel-mouthed gunman giving me a scare. It was
what he'd called me . . . *old?* A man, yes, but old? I
could tell you stories . . . A *bastard?* Are you joshing
me, son? I could tell you stories about my daddy for a
full month and never stop but to take a drink! I was
good and mad is why I was shaking!

"Now, boys," I said, looking over my left shoulder at
my sons, "there's a lesson to be learned here. I've been
telling you for the longest time that you got to respect your
elders. And ary you can't find it in you to respect
your elders, why, you'd damn sure better learn to respect your betters."

The Winchester was in my right hand. I wasn't all that
good with my left hand, but at the moment I was too
damn mad to care. The oak tree hadn't taken notice of
the way I was balling up my fist, which was all to my
advantage when I swung and made contact with him. I
was aiming for his jaw, but what I hit was the side of his
neck, an action that damn near made his eyes fall out of
their sockets. He staggered back, a shocked look on his
face. The shock changed to fear by the time I'd stuck
that brass boy into his throat.

"You move anywhere but backwards, sonny, and I'll

pull the trigger on this gun," I said, pushing hard against his Adam's apple as he took one step back, me one forward.

That put me right in between his fellow gunmen, both of them starting to reach for their guns before freezing as solid as a mountain lake in the dead of winter. A quick glance over my shoulder verified what I already knew. Between my boys and the Juarezs, those fellows were outgunned two to one. It was pistols and rifles they were looking at and second thoughts they were having about this being their last day above the earth. The chief, he sat there just shaking his head back and forth while he took a gander at his men, seeing they were gone beaver if they didn't make the right moves. Long John, I didn't see him anywhere.

The oak tree, his face had turned white as a sheet. I gave him one last nudge with my rifle before he turned away, upchucking whatever it was he'd had for breakfast.

"I've never seen him before in my life," Jared Watts said, making an appearance.

"Jared Watts, you're a lying sonofabitch." I said it hard and loud, wanting all of them to hear, wanting to push him four ways from Sunday so he'd go for that pistol he wore. Hell, he was standing on flat ground, thirty yards off from the man Diah had shoved off his horse who was now spread-eagled flat on the ground. Now, hoss, you try telling me you recognize a man's face from that far off in the position this one was, why, you'd likely find me saying the same thing to you!

Jared Watts just smiled. He had more patience than I'd given him credit for and it only made me the madder.

"No, Hooker, you're not going to get a rise out of me." I hate people like that, acting high and mighty like they were right next to God when the whole of creation came about. It was time to put a hitch in his git along. I pulled the small bottle out of my pocket, the one Long John had handed me after telling his story.

"We'll see about that," I said, holding the bottle up for him to see. At one time it might have contained whiskey for a man who was sharing a cold night with

Mother Nature, but it didn't now. Me, I was betting Jared Watts knew what it did contain. I strode toward a water trough, pulling the cork out of the bottle with my teeth, spitting it out as quickly as I did. "I'll just add a slosh to your drinking water."

"NO!!" Any coolness he had was gone now and I knew I could believe Long John's story. He gulped hard, knowing the tables were turned now, that I had him by the short hairs. But he tried anyway. "I don't want any whiskey in that water."

"Horse apples, Watts! What you mean is you don't want any *poison* in your water." I poured the contents of the bottle onto the ground. "That's what your man here was trying to do to one of our watering holes when he got caught."

Watts' face was turnip red, and this time it was him who was doing the shaking. I'd called his hole card and caught him running a bluff. He wanted to kill me in the worst way, no doubt about it. But he also knew he'd never live to know whether the lead he threw my way did me in or not.

The silence was filled with more tension than I cared for, but Watts backed down, turned to go back to his quarters. Me, I wasn't finished yet.

"Watts!"

He stopped and turned to face me.

"Anything out of the ordinary happens to me or my men . . . I'll come after you. Ain't going to ask no questions; just going to come after you. Understand?" I spat out.

He didn't say a word, simply walked away. Yet, somehow, I knew I hadn't seen the last of the man or his bunch.

I was about to grab the reins to my horse when I realized how quiet it was. Something was missing, something that had been there when we rode in. The horse, that's what it was. And the whip. Both were silent now. A quick gander at that far corral and I saw Long John walking the mustang, petting it and patting it and getting a friendly nudge in return. Then I saw a man, likely the one who'd originally had the whip in his hand when we rode in. He was on the other side of the corral, and from ground level all I could see were his head and shoulders and what looked like a pistol he was bringing down at arm's length.

Long John was gone beaver and there wasn't a damn thing I could do about it!

"Sonofa—"

If anyone was listening to me, they never heard the last part of that. It was drowned out by the sharp crack of Eagle Feather's rifle as he shot the pistol from the man's hand. It impressed even me, and I didn't impress easy.

"That's mighty fine shooting, chief," I said.

"Damn right," was all he said, nodding his head once. For a man of few words, he put the right ones to use real well. And in a land where some men let their guns do their talking for them, why, he held a real to-the-point conversation with that long gun of his.

Long John went back to soothing the mustang, which had become jittery from the gunfire. Walking it to the edge of the corral, he flung the large wooden gate—also in need of repair—halfway open. It looked like he was having his own conversation with the animal before bringing a huge hand down on the mustang's flank. The wild horse shook its head the way a human will do when feeling a chill, then was gone out onto the prairies. Long John, he had a real pleasant smile about him when he came back to mount his own horse.

"You thinking what I'm thinking, Pa?" Matthew asked.

"You bet, son," I said, giving him a nod as I mounted up. "I do believe we found us our man."

Chapter 8

Long John must have figured something was up once he saw the sigh of relief on everyone's face after Matthew and I had exchanged words. My own boys knew they'd be riding herd on a string of remounts for each man in the outfit if we didn't get a wrangler for the job. Bud and Jorge, well, let's just say that they were getting to know me well enough to figure they'd be second choice on my list for the job. Hell, they were the only other ones I could count on. The chief, he just took it all in, watching and waiting the way many an Indian will do. It was Long John that let his curiosity be known.

"Should I assume you were referring to me when you said that?" he asked, aiming the question at me and Matthew. I glanced over my shoulder, making sure there was a good bit of distance between my back and Jared Watts and his crew before I felt comfortable enough to continue the conversation. I'd learned long ago that you don't turn your back on a rattlesnake just because you've stood him off.

"That's right, son." I let my horse slow to a walk, giving him his head for the moment. The others did the same, Matthew cutting back from my side to make room for Long John.

"Do you think you might want to let me in on the secret?" He was polite as could be now. It was the kind of politeness you come to expect from a man servant on one of those fancy Tom Jefferson plantations. Not that I'd been to all that many of them, you understand.

"You worked right fine with that mustang back there," I said, seeing if he'd pick up the drift.

"That was a fine mount. He deserved better than that whip that was being laid to him."

"Wouldn't argy it for a minute, no, sir." I had yet to face the man, looking straight ahead as I spoke. "Do much of it?"

"Work with horses? Sure do." I could hear it in his voice before I glanced over to see the happiness come to his face. Mustangs were a subject he enjoyed, sort of like guns with Matthew. Or maybe it was because there was a bit of the mustang in the man I was looking at. Maybe that was their kinship. Whatever the link between them, that wild mustang and this free man had a way of getting along with one another, of that I was sure.

"I could use a good wrangler," I said, getting it out in the open. "Ary you figure you could work with this motley bunch of misfits." I said it loud enough for both the Juarezs and my own boys to hear. Tom Lang and his men would never consider us to be more than hired help or outright pilgrims when it came to pushing cattle, the whole lot of us, but he'd need every bit of help he could get from all the men who were available to him.

Long John grinned, raising a curious black eyebrow. Still, I had the feeling that he wasn't all that surprised. "Well, now, I don't have any immediate plans." Again that careless shrug. "Why don't you fill me in on what this job entails."

He was getting their attention, I'll say that. Mine, too. Most people didn't figure on hearing the kind of vocabulary this man was using coming from someone wearing black skin.

"Getting ready to push a bunch of longhorns north any day now. Got most everything I need 'cepting a wrangler. You take this on, you'll be taking care of every man's string of horses on this drive. The others, they'll be herding cattle. Your job is to herd the horses. Have 'em ready when they're needed. Pays the same as the rest of the hands get. From what I hear, it's 'bout the most thankless job to have. You'll get ridden just like you was a hoss, made fun of, and given a hard time from the day you start 'til the end of trail." I paused, cocked a weary eye at him. "You think you can take all that?"

He burst out laughing in a voice that almost became a roar. This time it was the rest of us that were surprised. We all gave one another questioning glances, not a one of us sure what was going on or why. Finally, he calmed down and gave me a smile, shaking his head.

"Mister Hooker, I've been putting up with the kind of adversity you describe for the better part of my life," he said. "The work may be hard, but I think I can take nearly anything else you throw at me. Yes, Mister Hooker, I think I can handle it."

Made me feel like a fool for a minute there. Here I was, talking about everything the man would be running up against in the job he'd be taking and not even considering what his background was or his qualifications or anything. I leaned a bit closer to him, lowered my voice.

"Reckon I seem like a desperate man, son, but—"

"Actually, I'm glad you said what you did," he interrupted. "You were addressing me as a man, Black Jack, and believe me, that alone means a lot." He smiled, likely knowing he'd spared me having to swallow some pride, which was just as important to me as being treated like a man was to him. A body has to have something to hold on to inside himself. Gets you through the rough parts, if you know what I mean.

The ride back to camp was relatively quiet after that. It was pushing noon when those cottonwoods came into view. It was also about then that I remembered something I'd been meaning to ask Long John from the start. Fact is, we were riding into camp as I said it.

"Just where did you say it was you got my name?"

"Well, it wasn't me exactly," he replied in as close to

a manner of embarrassment as I'd seen him come to. "It was Eagle who—"

"Brown gargle's on the fire, boss," Latch Key said for all to hear. All but the chief, that is. To the Indian he said, "Injun coffee is over there," pointing to what was likely a near empty pot of coffee, probably with luke-warm contents. I was finding out that it was the custom of these cowmen to feed any Indian who came to camp a diluted cup of coffee. A cowhand wouldn't have touched it, but some of the Indians were simply beggars, happy with what little they got from these camps. But I'll tell you one thing, hoss, that frown that came to Eagle Feather's forehead upon hearing the cook's comment gave me a pure indication that I might have another war on my hands.

I don't know how Maria got through all of this without throwing in her two bits worth, but she did, standing there next to the chuck wagon and watching it all. Tom Lang and his crew were on the other side of the camp, eating their noon meal. Somehow, I wasn't all that sure Lang would settle for the simple act of eating right now. I was right.

"Letting any old body into camp now, are you, Hooker?" he said.

"We need a wrangler. I found a man who can do the job. He ain't done nothing yet to show me different."

"Ask me, you'll never see him do more than talk," Latch Key said. It wasn't that he didn't like the man, you understand, as much as not liking the *kind* of man Long John was. There's a whole bunch of ways you can say the word *prejudice*, you know.

Instinct and reflex action took hold of the camp about that time. Why, even the chief cocked that long gun of his. His thumb cocking that trigger was about all that moved, but it was enough to let anyone interested know that he'd dealt himself into this hand. Lang was already on his feet, and it wasn't long before the rest of his crew was, too. Their coffee cups and plates were on the ground; backing up their boss was part of their job and they were all prepared to go to the limit for him. Long

John, he didn't look any too happy at all. No, sir. And
you can believe I wasn't even going to ask him if he was
willing to back off. Like I said, a man's got to have
something to keep him going.

"You sure have one helluva way of showing appreciation, mister," Long John said through grit teeth. He was
staring at Latch Key when he said it. The cook, well, he
was doing his best to hold up his end in what was now
only a staring match. Anything or anybody else moved
and you could bet it was going to be war, plain and
simple.

These two were doing nothing more than waiting for it
to happen. But I had too much to do that day to fit dying
in along with it.

"What're you talking 'bout, John? Appreciation for
what?" I was talking to him all right, but my eyes were
roaming the rest of the camp, waiting for someone to
make the wrong move.

"The last time I saw you," Long John said, continu-
ing to glare at Latch Key, "you had a ghostly look on
your face and a rope around your neck. Of course, it
didn't stay attached to that cottonwood for long."

Latch Key's eyes got wide as the same thoughts ran
through his mind as did mine. His near hanging in town
the other day is what he was thinking about. That mys-
terious shot from the second storey window that cut
through that rope like a piece of lightning. Yup, he was
thinking the same thing I was. Guaranteed.

"I shoot more than hats," Eagle Feather said unex-
pectedly. His attention was focused on Maria. "Ask
him," he added, slowly leaning forward to look past
Long John at me.

When he said that, it all fell into place; the events of
that day. The first shot had saved Latch Key from
certain death by hanging, be it accidental or on purpose.
The second one had taken the hat off the head of the
man holding Maria hostage, and had rattled him enough
to give the rest of us the time we needed to lay him low.
I had no doubts now about how everything had taken
place. From the surprised looks on the faces of the cook

and his wife, I'd say they were putting it all together at about the same time. But that deathly silence lasted only a few seconds longer

"I was just about to throw these out," Maria said, picking up the near empty pot of old coffee grounds. "If you'd like coffee, I'll get some extra cups." She made sure she took in both Long John and the chief when she said it.

Lang's men went back to their meal, but Lang himself stood there, stubborn as a Missouri mule. We dismounted and Maria returned with cups for all. She began pouring the hot liquid while each of the rest of us waited for someone else to speak. I'll tell you, son, if words were water right then I don't believe you'd find a dryer spot on this earth than that camp. Latch Key was still measuring up Long John, and Lang was just waiting to disrupt things again.

"Reckon I owe you more'n a cup of coffee," Latch Key said in a voice that wasn't the loudest you'd ever hear. Prejudice dies hard and that was evident in my cook's try at being thankful to a man whose race he'd likely looked down on most of his life.

"I was glad to help." Long John offered his hand in friendship, which, to some, might have been surprising. What was surprising to me was that Latch Key took it without hesitation. I got the feeling then that Long John had a lot more going for him than just a decent command of words. You can know every one of them, but they don't mean spit unless you can use them the right way. Hell, even Jim Bridger would tell you that, and he couldn't read or write! But he knew just the same.

"Long John, this here's Tom Lang," I said by way of introduction. "He rides herd on this outfit."

"Nice to meet you, Mister Lang," Long John said with a smile as he stuck out his hand. But Lang didn't respond. If anything, the look on his face turned more contemptible than it had been at first sighting the black man.

"It don't rub off, Tom," Latch Key said, raising the palm of his own hand. "See."

"No," Lang said, more to himself than anyone. "I ain't taking on no—"

"Ary I forgot to mention it, John, *I'm* the one who rides herd on Lang here," I said. Lang didn't like it, but then, that seemed to be the way of things between us by now. "Son," I said to him in a tone he didn't like much either, "you may be top dog out with that herd, but when it comes down to the *small* details in this outfit, like who stays and who goes, I'll have the say on it. And that's that." I was talking down to him like a father who's disappointed in his son and no grown man likes that, not even from his real father. Fact was, I damn sure didn't want Lang for a son, and I know good and well he would have hated my guts, even if I was his father.

"There *is* one thing, Black Jack," Long John said in that cautious manner people have of speaking when they haven't told you everything.

"Do tell."

"Eagle and I, we work together." It was all or nothing, the way he said it, and he'd stand by whatever decision was made. In the short time I'd known him, I could already sense certain things about the man and his character.

"How you gonna justify an Injun on the drive, Hooker?"

"Lang, when will you stop trying to make trouble?" I've got to tell you, hoss, I was getting tired of the man and his ways real quick. Fact is, I was about to answer my own question when the chief stopped talking to Maria a few paces away and made it to our little group in a handful of steps.

"You go up there?" he asked, pointing to the north.

"Yeah. Why?" Lang replied, still mad.

"You will need me."

"Not hardly, chief," the ramrod said. "I'm pushing cattle and you don't look to me to be all that good with cattle." He said it with an air of finality. Eagle Feather simply turned to speak with me, turning a deaf ear to the Texan.

"I am a Ute," he said proudly.

"Knew that when I first seen you ride up out there," I said, throwing a thumb over my shoulder. "Spent too long in the Shinin' Mountains not to learn the tribes I was living amongst."

"You were at the Walls." One thing about the people who were native to this land was that they didn't ask an awful lot of questions. Figure things out for themselves, they do. So what the chief said could have been a question, but it was more a statement. Trouble was I wasn't quite sure of what he was talking about. What walls? The expression on my face said the same thing, I reckon, for he added, "Adobe Walls. On the Canadian."

"Right." I nodded, now remembering exactly what it was he was talking about. It was near winter back in '64 that the Second New Mexico Volunteers had run into a thousand or two Kiowa and Comanche who didn't take kindly to us being in their territory. Must've been three-, maybe four-to-one odds against us, but we made it out, hides and all. Wasn't any big victory, unless you call pulling your own fat out of the fire a victory. Me, I'd been sort of an unofficial volunteer and guide in the whole mess. "Remember it well," I said.

"There was another man named John with you then."

"If there was, I don't recall him," I said, squinting as I tried to make my memory work right. But I couldn't conjure up this fellow.

"I talked with that John. He said you were a good man. Loud but good." I do believe it was the closest I'd come to seeing Eagle Feather smile. Nothing that would show on his lips, you understand. It was his eyes that said he enjoyed that description of me.

"What the hell does all that have to do with being on this trail drive?" Lang said, damn near exploding with impatience.

"Shut up, Lang," I said. I could talk business, too, and it came out hard. Lang didn't care.

"The hell I will!"

Eagle Feather took one step closer to the trail boss, putting them eyeball to eyeball. I'll tell you, hoss, the way both of them were setting to go at one another, why, I wasn't any too sure I wanted to get into this war. No, sir.

"You were at the Walls?" Eagle Feather asked him.

"No. I rode with Ben McCulloch during the war."

"I was at the Walls. We fought the Comanche. I do not like them. They are my people's enemy. When you go north, you will be attacked by the Comanche." The look on his face now said he had Lang by the short hairs. He nodded his head slowly up and down. "You will need me."

As abruptly as he had turned to face Lang, he returned his attention to me. To Eagle Feather, Lang was a forgotten man, although I had a strong notion that if the Texan had gone for his pistol, he'd have been *dead* and forgotten.

"When I talked with the other John, I also talked with Carson. You know Carson." Hell yes, I knew Kit Carson! All your memory and half of your brains would have to dribble out your ears before you'd forget that man! Small in size, he was, but he made up for it in all he'd done on that campaign. Fact is, if you didn't believe half of the stories about the man's exploits, why, you'd be a guaranteed believer once you fought with him at the Walls. Yes, I knew Carson. Knew him long before Adobe Walls, all the way back to the Shinin' Mountains.

"He says you are a good man. His word is good. That is why we came."

Eagle Feather had done all the talking he had in mind, I reckon, for he turned away and headed back across the camp to talk to Maria again.

"Well, boys, I do believe we've got us some work to do afore can't see," I said, trying to regain some control of the situation now that the powder keg had some water thrown on it, at least for the moment.

"Lang, you are in charge of getting this herd moving and keeping it moving when we get on the trail. John, your job is to keep us a decent string of horses," I said.

"What about Eagle?" John asked.

"Why, he's my Indian scout," I said with a smile.

That was good enough for Long John. Tom Lang—well, I reckon he'd had enough of tangling with a bear for one day. Both of them left to tend to their separate chores.

It wasn't that I needed an Indian scout, you understand, for I'd been doing that myself now for I don't know how long. I'd never admit it to anyone, but I was keeping the chief on hand so I'd have someone to talk over old times with if nothing else.

Chapter 9

It was the morning two days later that we started the drive. Tom Lang and the crew finished up their branding and Latch Key had all of the necessary supplies cached in his wagon. He'd even convinced Diah to invest in another wagon, a freight wagon for some extras he had in mind. That suited me fine, for I'd just told that brassy boy of mine to purchase some extra powder and ball for the outfit as well. I figured we could always use it.

My boys and the Juarez lads knew they'd be taking on trail driving jobs once we got underway, so only Latch Key, Maria, and I were in camp when that big mass of longhorns began to move. Long John was taking care of the remuda and Eagle Feather was someplace out front, looking for water holes and anything out of the ordinary. Me, I was giving the cook a hand getting all his equipment packed up so he could get out of here, too. After all, he had to beat us to the noon dry camp. More importantly, the *coffee* had better be there by the time the herd and the men working it showed up. If it wasn't, Latch Key would be out of a job.

"Something I've been meaning to ask you, boss," he said, never once stopping his work.

"What's that?"

"How come you had to wait as long as you did before you went looking for a cook? I sure can't picture Lang

62

fixin' sonofabitch stew without accidentally chopping part of his own self up in the process. If you know what I mean."

I laughed. "That's a fact. Lang don't seem to be much good for more than pushing cattle and men." I kicked some dirt onto the already dying flames. "Had a cook . . . and a wrangler."

"Quit on you, did they?"

"No," I said, drawing it out slow and cautious. "They died." That stopped both him and his wife in their tracks. Facing death is hard enough, but talking about it isn't much fun either.

"What happened to them?" Maria asked, a look of true concern on her face. "I mean how did they—"

"Cookie made the mistake of drinking his own coffee first. Everyone else was out on the roundup, but he and the wrangler were going to be the first ones to have at that coffee, I reckon. I found 'em dead, laying there by the fire, when I came in."

"But what caused it?" Latch Key suddenly seemed to have stopped caring about his utensils.

"I got rid of the cups and moved their bodies around some before the crew came in. Took my boot to the backs of their heads and kicked 'em right hard. Made it look like they'd gotten into a fight with one another and fell just right alongside wagon wheels and rocks to kill each other in the process. Told Lang and his boys I'd seen the end of it when I rode into camp but couldn't save 'em." If you've ever felt edgy about owning up to something, friend, then you know just how I was feeling. "Odd bird, Lang. Swallowed the whole line like some bigmouthed bass."

"But what happened? Was the coffee . . . poisoned?" Maria looked about ready to break out in tears, or at least run in the opposite direction from the one we were heading in.

"That's a fact." Then I gave them the shortened version of how I'd come across Long John and Eagle Feather and the run in I'd had with Jared Watts and his men.

"But how can you be sure they were poisoned?" she asked.

"Took that coffee pot out and got rid of most of the contents. Poured some into a little bowl and left it overnight just outside of camp. Now, I haven't seen many animals take to drinking that kind of liquid mud, but that ain't to say they don't get curious 'bout it."

"Get to the point," Latch Key said. He was getting more impatient the longer this story took to unfold.

"Found me a mean old cur next to that dish the next morning. Just as dead as those men were, he was." I nodded. "That brew was poisoned. Count on it."

"Then, why are you telling us now?" the woman said, a bit rattled from what she'd just heard.

"Well, lady, first off, he asked me," I said, nodding at her husband. "Second reason is that I ain't too keen on having it happen in this camp again. I figure if you know about it you might be able to keep an eye out for anything looks strange. You see, I figure we got us a spy of some sort in camp. That or the fella who planted that dash of poison was almighty quick, if he didn't belong to our outfit.

"One other thing you want to keep in mind, the both of you. I don't want word of this to leak out to anyone in the camp, understand?" By then I must've sounded a mite surly, but considering the seriousness of the situation and what could happen to the men, horses, and cattle on this drive, I don't believe that was out of line. Latch Key understood what I was getting at, but the woman had a mind of her own.

"And what if we don't keep it quiet?" she said defiantly. The way she stuck that jaw out, why, you'd think she'd made a living at being stubborn.

"I'll tell you what'll happen, darlin'." Hands on hips, I glared right back at her. "I figure old Latch Key knows there's a lot of truth in what my boy says about having one hellacious time trying to pick up your teeth off'n the ground with a couple of busted up hands. Makes it hard to tell your story, writing or speaking."

"You wouldn't dare do that to me!"

"Hell, no," I said, still talking as hard as I looked. "But I'll tell you something, little miss sweetness. You open your mouth about what I said here this morning, and I'll guarantee that the next time you show your bottom to someone, it'll by God be full of calluses!"

I had no more time to waste on a discussion that would lead nowhere. I turned and grabbed up my rifle, and crossed camp to my horse. All the time I was doing it, Maria was standing there, not quite believing what I'd said, mumbling, "You . . . you . . . you . . ." Flustered is what she was. Had so many names running through her head to call me that she couldn't figure out which one to pick first. Me, I wasn't quite through with her.

"Then they'll *know* you're a working woman," I added as I mounted up.

Her chest expanded enough to damn near bust open the work shirt she wore. At the same time her eyes bulged out of their sockets and her face got as red as a newly painted barn. She was past words now, heading for the bowie knife her husband had laid on the gate of the chuck wagon. But as quick as she was, Latch Key was quicker, his solid hand grasping her wrist and forcing the knife to drop to the ground. He wasn't too pleased with what I'd said, but I could see he wasn't about to try bucking the tiger either.

"Maybe you'd better leave while it's still safe, boss."

"Right. And mebbe you oughtta get this outfit up north for noon camp."

Mexican standoffs were getting to be the order of the day.

Hot-tempered as he was, I had to give Tom Lang credit for knowing what he was doing with the cattle and men on a trail drive. I'd meant just what I'd said about him being the boss when those longhorns were on the trail. Hell, he claimed to have been on a similar drive once before, taking these stringy looking creatures up north to Sedalia, Missouri. Wasn't long after the war ended, as I recall.

Lang was somewhere between my own boys when it

came to age, late twenties, maybe thirty. But you can bet that when I called his crew "boys," why, I meant just that. Most of them were younger than Diah, and he was only twenty-one or so. Still, they were men in their own eyes and I wouldn't begrudge them that. They made a big to-do about having served in the war, knowing cattle, and being a By-God-Texican. I understood it all, having gone through the same thing nearly forty years before up in the Shinin' Mountains. These lads, well, being in that war and surviving it was the highlight of their lives so far. They never spoke of the fact that they'd been on the losing side. Surviving, that was what it had all turned into, what they had to hang onto in this life. Like I said, everyone's got to have something to keep them going.

If you worked your way from the front of the herd to the back, it looked something like this. Each side was tended to by a "lead" or "point" man. For the most part they kept that herd from branching out up front. I could've sworn it looked like the front of the herd had taken the shape of an arrow, if you get my drift, the leader way out front while the rest followed. To hear Lang talk, this was the most honored place to be located on the drive. You had to have a good bit of responsibility to be placed in a lead position since those two men determined the course and direction of the drive that day. Naturally, Lang had a couple of his own youngsters out front when we started out. Honored or not, I had to wonder if being a lead man wasn't just a mite dangerous to boot, for these lads would be the first ones to face a head-on Indian attack or to cross a river. And let me tell you, son, crossing a river with a herd this size could be treacherous.

About one third of the way behind the lead man was the "swing" rider, and two thirds behind him the "flank" rider. These men kept the cattle in column. When the drive started up in the morning, it was the swing man's job to get those bunched cattle strung out in a column. Once that was done, if any of these thick-headed beasts decided to wander off, it was the swing and flank riders' job to keep them from going any farther and retrieving the critters. These positions were filled by the rest of Lang's boys and my own. It was also in this area of the herd that Lang could be most often found if you needed him. I reckon he was a bit fidgety about Matthew and Diah doing this kind of work, not knowing them like I did. They may not have been the cattlemen that Lang and his crew were, but I'll guarantee you they pick up on things right quick. Yes, sir.

The tail end of the herd was watched over by the "drag" rider. It was also the worst place to be on the drive if you gave a man his druthers. The drag rider had to be on constant lookout for those lame or lazy animals that fell back. It was his job to urge them on and keep the back end of this operation together. All of that might not seem so bad, and it wasn't. What made this position the worst one to work at was the fact that whoever did the job was going to be eating the dust of every one of those few thousand longhorns from can see to can't see. By the time the day was over, the drag rider would figure cookie'd better have found him at least a lake to camp by because his throat was as parched as the Mojave Desert and his lungs so full of dust he could hardly breathe. If you haven't been following this process of elimination, I'll add here that it was those Juarez lads who got appointed to this position on the drive—at least for that first day.

The only thing behind them was the remuda that Long John was in charge of. It must've had over a hundred horses in it, but the black man knew how to handle them. I had a notion that some of those fancy minded folks from back east would have raised hell at having fought a war to free the Negro, only to find Long John working at the back end of the drive. But that had nothing to do with anything out here. No, sir. He'd signed on as a wrangler and that's the position he took on this long drive.

During the mornings the cook and his wagon would follow the drive, staying off to the side to keep from being caught up in the massive cloud of dust those

longhorns could create. But after a noon camp of serv-
ing up coffee, cold biscuits, and jerked beef to the men,
he would move out ahead of the herd. He'd keep on
going until he found the place the trail boss had settled
on; one that had a decent supply of water and wood for
the night. That was where he'd start fixing supper for
the men. One important part of his set up that afternoon
would be the position in which he located his wagon. To
anyone else it might not seem like much, but the unwrit-
ten rule was that the tongue of that chuck wagon pointed
in the direction the drive would begin the next morning.

Oddly enough, it went pretty well that first day.

"Can't believe it went this smoothly," I said to Lang
when everyone had gotten fed and the night hawks had
been posted. The night hawks were the two men who
slowly circled the herd at night riding in opposite directions. Everyone pulled a two-hour shift at it except the
cook.

"That Davy sure can sing to 'em," Lang said, ignor-
ing me.

"Gonna snow tomorrow, you think?"

"Yeah," he replied, still thinking about the young
night hawk out there. I thought I actually saw some kind
of pleasantness in his eyes at that moment, but it didn't
last long. "Huh? Snow? What are you talking about,
Hooker?" The frown was back and the bad disposition
with it.

"I said it went pretty well today."

"All things considered, yes." He drank some coffee
before throwing me a hard glance. "Just don't get too
comfortable, Hooker." He drank the rest of the coffee,
then shook the cup out.

"Oh?"

"It's only the first day."

He was right.

Chapter 10

They squinted when they woke up the next morning, not believing what they saw, but every man jack of them woke up quietly and that was the important thing. After what had happened with Tom Lang and Maria the day before, most of the camp had been wondering how we were going to get through the rest of the drive from one morning to the next without stampeding the cattle. I know it had crossed my mind. But from the look of it Maria was picking up on things right quick. Yes, sir.

What the camp woke up to just before dawn was the soft sound of heavy spurs being dragged across the ground. Just loud enough for the men to hear without the cattle noticing, it was. What caught most of these men off guard was looking up to see Maria dragging her tiny feet along inside a pair of boots that looked to be the size of the whole Texas navy, from one side of the camp to the other. I breathed a bit easier seeing it, knowing that one of my problems had been taken care of. What gave me an itch was seeing Maria return the smiles of those fresh awakened men as they took a long gander at her. She was giving them notions they'd likely only dreamed about so far and I had no room for that on the drive.

Neither did Tom Lang.

"All right, you crow bait," he growled from his posi-

69

tion next to the chuck wagon, "put them eyeballs back
in and get a move on it. You're burning daylight."

"But it's not even daylight yet, señor," Bud said,
rubbing his eyes.

"That's why you two are riding drag on this drive."
He leaned over, coffee cup in hand, that meaner-than-
hell look about him. I was beginning to believe he was
born with it. "In this outfit you're gonna start work long
before the sun comes up. And I'll guarantee that if you
want to get paid at trail's end, you're gonna do your
share of working after old sol goes down. That goes for
the rest of you pilgrims, too," he added, throwing an
equally harsh glare at my sons.

"Let him get it out of his system, boys," I said,
shaking my head at Matthew and Diah as they prepared
to get up and beat the stuffing out of Lang. Lang didn't
like that at all, something I was getting used to about the
man. Hell, it seemed like he had it in for everyone in
camp except his own boys.

"You think that was easy yesterday, do you, Hooker?"
he said, turning his wrath on me. If anything, he got
meaner. "We went all of *six* miles yesterday in no formation any decent cowman would ever use. Why, those
damn critters was so bunched up I'm surprised they
didn't stampede and kill the whole lot of you!" Here
again he was talking strictly to me, my boys, and the
Juarez lads. He stopped a moment, took us all in, then
remembered he was shy a couple of hands for what he
had to say. Looking around briefly, he didn't see them.
"Where's Monsure and old Pheasant Feather, or whatever his name is?" he demanded.

Tom Lang was letting everyone know that he was
taking charge of things, all of which may have been fine
with his own men, but didn't set too well with the rest of
us. So far the highlights of my day had been watching
the woman walk away from me in those boots and the
coffee I'd had.

"Should I assume you're speaking to us?" I could
have sworn that Long John and the chief had been there
at the edge of camp when Maria did her walking, but

apparently they'd slipped out as soon as they wakened. Neither one of them looked too awful happy as they stepped into the light of the campfire. It was hard telling whether it was the lack of coffee or Lang's spouting off that made them look that way, but if I had to be on it, I'd place my money on Lang being the instigator.

"Hell, yes." Lang wasn't letting up, not one bit. "Anyone talks the way you do for being who you are needs a label like Monsure."

"I see," was all Long John said. Calm as could be. But you know something, hoss, I had a feeling that calm reply rattled Lang more than the man going for a gun or going toe to toe with him would have.

"Well, here's something else you can see, mister. You don't do no night hawking, but you're damn sure gonna work for your pay. Today we're gonna start *moving* these longhorns, and I mean moving 'em. From now until we get these mangy things to the buyers, I want at least a half dozen fresh mounts ready for the crew at noon camp. Got it . . . boy?" That last word was as hard and ugly as Lang's look.

"Now, look here, gents," Diah said, taking a step forward. "I never had any use for that War Between the States and I've had my fill of Indian fighting for a while—"

"I'll get to you in a minute," Lang replied, giving Diah that same hard look before throwing it back at Long John.

"Don't push your luck," Long John said. He was getting just a mite testy, and there wasn't a man in camp that would blame him. "You'll have your mounts, Lang. Every day. Rain, shine, hail . . . hell, I don't care if it snows! You'll have them." What he said wasn't anywhere close to a statement. By God, what Long John was talking was a bonified guarantee! And the way he said it let everyone in camp know he'd live up to it. Not just Lang, but everyone. The lad had sand, I'll give him that. It was the kind of challenge Tom Lang wasn't quite ready for so he turned his attention to Eagle Feather.

"Hooker says he wants you riding out ahead, scouting, chief," he said. "Well, you do just that. And while you're at it, keep you an eye out for flat land and water where we can bed down the herd at day's end. Same goes for you as I said to Monsure here. I don't give a damn if I don't see you again 'til trail's end, chief, long as we got water and flat land by can't see.''

"And if I find none?"

"Start praying you'll find some before I find you.'' Still harsh, still mean, he was.

Eagle Feather took enough long strides to bring him face to face with Tom Lang. The Texan was a bit taller than the Indian, but that didn't make any difference, not to the Ute. Believe me, son, I know.

"You make big mistake, white man. Eagle Feather is my name." With one motion his hand swept over the top of his head, taking off the flat brimmed hat he wore. When the hand came to a halt, it held the hat at an angle where it would be impossible for Tom Lang to miss seeing the one lone feather that stuck in the hat band. "*Eagle Feather,*" the Indian said. You can call it pride if you like, but I'm here to tell you that there was a death warrant being issued by that man in the way he said those words. Tom Lang, he was gone beaver if he challenged this fellow again. Fact is, I'd say breathing was a chancy proposition at the moment.

"Big mistake." Slowly, Eagle Feather shook his head, as if to pity the man and his ways. Then, without a word, the hat was back in place and he took a step around Lang, stopping at my side. "Big wind comes early this morning," he said in that low voice of his.

"Ain't that the truth." I gave him a smile, to let him know I knew what he was talking about. Then he was gone.

Talking tough never got a man much more than a blister on his lip, the way I figure it. But Lang, why, I would've been surprised if he didn't have him a full callous on his mouth by the time he got through. And he wasn't through yet.

"Less'n God Almighty stands in our way, we're moving these animals a minimum of ten miles a day, fifteen if we can do it," he said, the furrow in his brow growing deeper. "Understand?"

"You ask much of a hired hand, señor," Bud said.

"I ain't asking *nothing*, chili, I'm *telling*." Now, hoss, I don't know what big mistake the chief had been talking about, but I'll tell you that those last words were another one. I'd already seen the mad that could build in those Juarez boys if you pushed them enough. Having seen it I also knew that the sparks in their eyes might just turn into fire coming out the end of those short guns they packed. I'd gauge Bud was giving it two seconds worth of thought before he figured on killing Lang. To my surprise, it was Matthew who stepped in. Sort of.

"Dropped your glove there, Lang," he said while taking one quick step toward the man, By the time Lang had looked down and realized that he'd been tricked and was looking back up at Matthew while going for his gun . . . well, it was too late. You show me where it says that just because something is the oldest it can't work proper.

Matthew brought a hard right around that caught the trail boss off guard and sent him back a step or two before he fell to the ground. The shock of the blow made him forget about the business with the gun for a moment as he lay there shaking his head. At the same time three of Lang's men brought their own guns out, only to be faced by those six-guns the Juarez boys were toting. Another Mexican standoff! Damn, but I was getting tired of them. I tossed the empty cup to Maria and took a few steps to where Tom Lang lay, trying to gather his senses.

"Put the guns away, children," I said to the whole lot of them, just like someone's daddy. At first there was some consternation amongst them, every one of them hesitating a moment, likely thinking it would be unmanly to give in. But when I said, "Put the damn things away!" in a mite louder voice, they did. Just between you and me, there's an art to getting your point across like that. You put a crusty edge to your voice that sounds like it came right off one of those fancy glaciers the scientists talk about. Then you toss in a look that guarantees hellfire if they don't give in. Works every time.

"Now that you've had your before breakfast nap, Lang, mebbe you'll want to think twicet afore you run that mouth of yours like it was the far end of the Mississippi emptying into the gulf," I said as the man silently arose. Real quiet now, he was. "Too many naps and you ain't gonna get a lick of work done, son. Bad for the jaw, too, the way you go about it."

Lang instructed two of his men to go out and relieve Slim and Davy when they were through eating, and told the third to get him some grub.

"You might as well get yours, too, before the cookie throws it out," he said to the rest of us. Just a mite tamer. "But when you do, set your git up end down right here. I still got talking to do and you still got listening to do."

What his palaver amounted to was how he wanted the drive run. He'd let us have our way the day before to see what we knew about trail driving, all of which was minimal compared to the natural born knowledge of any Texan. About midway through his speech, we were joined by Davy and Slim, both looking tired and dreary eyed. They'd just come off the last watch, the one no one particularly cared to catch for there would be no rest for them except those few precious minutes they had to eat and find a fresh mount.

"You boys feel up to being my point men?" As tired as they appeared, hearing the boss speak those words gave them a new burst of energy. Like I said, being the lead man was quite an honored position on a trail drive.

"Sure thing, Tom."

"You bet, boss."

"Good." Lang actually smiled briefly. "You're the best I've got." That made them eat that much faster, wanting to get on the trail again. I don't know if they noticed the looks of concern on our faces, but Lang did. He knew why, too. After all, Slim might have been closer to Diah's age, but it was a sure bet that Davy was a youngster.

"Look, I know they're young, but when I say they're the best I've got, I mean just that. They grew up in this country and they know ranching and cattle and how to move 'em." Lang paused a moment to swallow some coffee before returning our looks with one of his own. "Besides, they rode with me and Ben McCulloch. I can count on 'em."

"And you can't count on us?" Diah asked. He was saying what all of us were thinking.

"You're gonna have to prove yourself to me, fellas," he said, standing up and draining the rest of his coffee. "I know those boys out there. Way things been going, I ain't so sure I want to know you." Right sandy for a man who was standing there facing five men by his lonesome. "Only way it's gonna work from my end of it is if you take orders from me out on that trail. I know what I'm doing. Been through it before."

When that didn't wash and all he had standing before him was the same bunch of men getting angry at him, he turned to me.

"Look, Hooker, maybe you'll understand. You're a mountain man, right?"

I nodded suspiciously. "Spent some time in the Shinin' Mountains."

"Well, after you'd been out there a few seasons and you had some greenhorn join up with you, you didn't put him in charge of setting the traps or breaking the trails, did you?"

"Hell, no!" I exploded, shocked at the man's audacity. "Why, them young whelps was nowhere near knowing all that I did!"

"There!" He poked a stubby finger through the air at me. "That's just what I'm talking about! I'll guarantee you, Hooker, that as young as those lads are out there, they've forgotten more about cattle than you'll ever know." When he saw the ire coming to my face, he decided to amend what he'd said. "Just like you've forgotten more about those trapping days than I'll ever know."

"You've made your point," I conceded.

"That being the case, here's how it's gonna be. Davy and Slim ride point for me, just like I said. Bob and Charlie will be riding swing. Frank and you, Guns, are gonna be my flank men. You two have the drag," he said to the Juarez boys. "I'll give you some advice though. If you don't want your lungs so full of dust, pull up them neckerchiefs over your faces. You'd be hard pressed to be taken for a bank robber out here." He spread out one arm, taking in a large expanse of open land. Everyone chuckled except the Juarez boys.

"Diah, what I've got in mind for you is a bit of this and that," Lang continued. "You're good with that rope, so you can help out here and there as is needed. Understand?"

"Sure." My boy nodded. "So much for this, now what about that."

"Well, seeing as it's your money that's invested in this lash up, you'd likely agree that you oughtta be the one to say how it's spent." Diah nodded. "That being the case, when cookie says he's getting low on provisions, I want you to get up there past the chief and find us a town and get them extra supplies. Won't be much to it. I know most of 'em along the route," Lang said.

"What about me?" I asked.

"I hope you can count, Hooker, cause that's what you and me are gonna start out doing every morning from here on out." I gave him a cautious glance, but he'd already turned his attention to the others. "By the way, boys, except for the drag end of this drive, I don't want those steers bunched up no more than three abreast when we're moving 'em. They don't like being crowded any more than you do."

That was all he had to say, calling a final halt to the conversation just like that. "Break camp, cookie," was all he mumbled as he went to his horse.

I didn't have much choice but to follow him to find out what he had in mind. When we got to the north side of the herd, I got a glimpse of what would be happening every morning from here on out.

"Head 'em up," Lang said in that booming voice of

his. With those words, Davy and Slim, the point riders, cut out the leaders, the two or three cattle who would be leading the drive, and nudged them over to the trail. The other longhorns would follow them. "Stay right there and start counting, Hooker," Lang added before moving his own mount to the far side of the leaders, facing me. Then, in that booming voice again, "String 'em out."

They milled around and milled around, those longhorns, not sure of what to do or where to go until they spotted a handful more of their kind leaving the herd. It seemed like a slow process, but it worked, and by the time the sun was upon us we had them strung out quite a ways. Each set of riders left to take their position on the drive as the string of cattle lengthened.

While that parade was forming, Tom Lang and I were getting a tally count of just how many head we had. The idea was to compare today's count with yesterday's and see how many of the herd we might have lost or gained in one day's time. To do the counting, Lang used an old shot pouch he had filled with pebbles, putting one in the big pocket of his coat for each one hundred head he counted. Me, I had two pockets full of cartridges, so I used them instead of the pebbles. When we had finished counting, we compared our amounts, and came up with the same number.

"That's trail count, Hooker," Lang said when we'd moved out of the way of the drag riders and their cloud of dust. "Some will do it when they feel like it, but I've got five ranchers back there who are counting on me, so we'll do it every day. Unless, of course, you have some objection." He had sounded right civil in his speaking except for that last sentence. It was then he'd dropped into the tone of voice I didn't care for. Never could stand a man looking down on me, especially when I was taller than him.

"Nope, don't mind a-tall, Lang." I had to admit that Tom Lang knew his job, was, in fact, good at it from what I'd seen so far on this trail drive. But he needed to be taught a lesson his own self. "Things would go a lot better ary we started working together, what with us all having the same goal in mind.''

"That's the damn truth.''

His attitude and the way he expressed himself, that's what it was that bothered me.

"Tell me something, Lang,'' I said.

"What's that?''

"Gamble much, do you?''

"I've sat in on a poker game or two. Why?''

"Ever heard of thimblerigging?'' I knew he had. Hell, it was one of the oldest con games in existence. Didn't matter if you used a walnut shell or a thimble, the game was older than the hills. I never did find mention of it in the Good Book, but I wouldn't be a bit surprised if that wasn't how Adam lost out to Eve way back when.

"Sure. Say, what are you getting at?'' I had his curiosity aroused now, had him wondering what I was about. He'd stepped far enough into the trap to let it spring, so I did.

"Oh, nothing,'' I said in as nonchalant a way as possible. "It's just that I heard it all originated with you Texans.''

That was it. These Texas people had been through some hard times since old Stephen Austin took his original three hundred down here in the twenties. But they'd survived and made a place of it and if there was one thing I knew they cherished, it was their pride in being called Texans. Tarnish that and you could start a war, which is what I'd just about done. By the time he had his six-gun out and pointed at me, he'd rattled off a line of cuss words as long as our string of cattle. But I didn't figure him for being the kind who would pull the trigger on that gun unless he deliberately wanted to start a stampede—and lose his reputation as a decent trail boss.

I smiled. Then I frowned at him. Hard.

"Put the damn thing away, Tom.''

"I oughtta . . .'' He started again, but he was so damn mad that he couldn't get it out.

"How's it feel?'' I asked, acting as though nothing had happened.

"What?" I had him confused now.

"Why, being insulted, of course." I leaned across the saddle and grinned like the cat that ate the canary. "Thought you'd like to know how Bud and Jorge felt this morning afore they went for their guns. The chief and John, too, I reckon." I cocked a warning eye at him and added, "I wouldn't count 'em out yet. Like you said, this drive just started."

I pulled back on my reins and put the heels to my mount, leaving the tall Texan scratching his head as he put away his gun. But you know something, hoss? I do believe I got my point across to Tom Lang that morning. Yes, sir.

Chapter 11

You might say we had an uneasy truce after that talk, Tom Lang and me, but I'll tell you, son, it was more like an old bull keeping an eye on a younger one who has *his* eye on taking over the herd. As for us outsiders catching onto what these Texas boys claimed to have been doing since the day after they were born, well, we didn't do too badly. Caught on right quick, we did.

We'd wake up to Maria taking her morning stroll in those oversized boots of Latch Key's, splash some water in our eyes if there was that much to spare, and go about the day's work, knowing that it would be can't see when we quit that day, just like it was when we got up.

One thing you learned out here was how to tell an easterner from a man who'd been out west for awhile. Easy as pie, if you think about it. It was all in how a man got dressed, which may sound strange, but was a verifiable fact. A man on the frontier, why, he dressed from the top down, while it was just the other way around for a fancified easterner. First thing a man out here did when he got through rubbing his eyes was slosh on his hat. Now, hoss, maybe that seems odd to you, but our breed—even these young Texas lads—felt flat out *naked* without something covering our top knot. Most would rattle out their boots next, to get out any strange visitors who might have taken up residence overnight. Not Davy, though. After putting his hat on, he would check the loads of his six-gun and *then* put his boots on. The boy got me curious.

"Expecting visitors, are you?"

"You might say," he replied with a smile.

"There something I should know?" I asked next, my thoughts immediately running to Jared Watts and his crew. I reckon I hadn't gotten to where I really trusted these Texas boys yet, having only been on the trail with them a couple of weeks now.

The boy smiled again.

"Not unless you're having the same trouble with tarantulas that I am." I frowned at him some. My mind might have been a mite foggy for that early in the morning, but what I'd heard so far was just plain confusing. Davy must've noticed. He smiled again when he said, "Why, Mister Hooker, I woke up one morning some time back and had to fight one of those darn things to get my boot back. So big he near carried my boot off for his own self."

Tarantulas were one of the strange visitors that a man kept an eye out for when he shook out those boots of his. Great big, hairy spiders is what they were. I reckon they were about as curious as humans, what with their always winding up in a body's boots. I sure don't think it was the odor of a man's feet that attracted them; or maybe it was at that. One thing you found out quick unless you sent them scurrying was that they didn't like having their sleep interrupted anymore than anyone else does. They had an annoying bite that stung like hell and did nothing to add to your disposition.

Davy's comment brought some laughter from the other men.

"Son," I said with a smile, "I got a feeling I just been stung."

That brought some more laughter, an old bastard like me being taken by this youngster's story. But there was something about the boy that made him likable and I found myself as drawn to him as the others were. Believe me, after putting up with Tom Lang and his stone face for as long as I had to each day, seeing the smile on this boy's face was a relief. I had a feeling that hearing his voice singing to those longhorns at night made the camp rest as at ease as those cattle.

As for strange visitors, well, son, tarantulas weren't the only ones we had. A few more showed up later on that afternoon. They were about as bothersome as a tarantula, but they only had two feet.

The herd had been a day without water already and Tom Lang was getting concerned about it. Not that I blamed him. Hell, there wasn't any use in driving cattle to market if the only thing you had when you got there was jerked beef on the hoof with the hide on. You'd likely wind up paying someone to take the critters off your hands if they were in that sad a shape. And none of us wanted that. So Lang, in his concern, had asked me to ride ahead and make sure cookie was setting up camp in the right place. Like I say, it was midafternoon so I wasn't in all that much of a hurry.

Two of them came riding right at me, straight out of the northeast. I was away from the herd by then, so the only distraction I had was them. And I'll tell you, hoss, if distracting me was what they had in mind, they did a whale of a job of it. I pulled up the reins on my horse and took to studying them, wondering were they renegade or peaceful. Looked like white men, which it turned out they were. But there weren't just two of them.

Their compadres rode in from the sides, sort of boxing me in. One from the rear and one each from the left and right of me. Must've been their idea how to have a captive audience.

"How do, gents," I said when they'd gotten close up. The two to my front weren't much more than medium build and plain-looking, but I'd learned long ago that you didn't have to look ugly to act twice that bad. No, sir. Why, I recall a fellow who was uglier than sin and nice as could be . . . but that's another canyon. So far no one had pulled a gun, which I took to be a good sign. Who knows, maybe this was just the cautious way folks had in these parts. "What can I do for you?" I asked.

"Getting on in the afternoon," the rider to my right said. Now this one could be trouble. Or maybe he was the ugly duckling of the outfit. Not that his features were all that misplaced, you understand. It's just that he talked with a sneer and had an overbearing attitude. Never could stand that in a person.

I took a slow gander at the sun over the opposite shoulder, also glancing at the silent rider on my left side. Take him out of the saddle and he'd have to stand on a soap box to talk with you eye to eye, he was that short.

"Wouldn't argy with you 'bout that," I allowed.

"I'm Lem Cordova," one of the men to my front said. The smile he gave me was more forced than natural. Something else I knew right away. Lem might have been what his mama named him, but I'd bet a dollar he wasn't the owner of that last name, not by a long shot. I had yet to see anyone of Mexican decent who would embarrass his ancestors by wearing one of those back east bowler hats like this fellow had on.

"This land is mine. All of it," he said.

"That a fact. Just paying a neighborly call then, are you?" I said. Of late I'd been finding it increasingly harder to sound like I was trying to be pleasant, especially when I didn't feel that way at all.

"In a manner of speaking." Still polite, still forcing that smile. "You're with the cattle drive, aren't you?"

"Yup. Why do you ask?" Looking at his face, I wondered if he hated this play acting as much as I did. He did, I reckon, for the smile disappeared and the cordial voice turned to one of pure business.

"Let's put our cards on the table, friend," he said. "The fact of the matter is that I charge a dollar a head to all those crossing my land with a herd." His face took on a frown and his voice turned hard. "Before that sun sets, you're going to give me a dollar for each head of cattle you intend to drive through my land. I'll take payment now," he added, glancing at the bulging pocket of my buckskin jacket.

"Talking to the wrong person, *friend*," I said, pulling out a handful of cartridges. "You want money you'll

have to talk to the cookie. He's the one keeps it for the
boss, you know. Boss oughtta be with him now, come to
think of it.'' I was talking faster than usual, trying to act
like I was a bit nervous about the whole situation. The
fellow before me was play acting a mite, and two can
play at that game. Put all my cards on the table? Listen,
hoss, I know better than that. So for the moment I
worked on my own diversion, all the time trying to
figure out how to get out of this mess.

"What's the matter, old man," the loudmouth on my
right said, the one with a sneer about him, "you edgy or
something?" If you're thinking there was hatred in my
eyes when I looked his way, you're right.

"Don't give me that look, old man," he added, slowly
moving his mount toward me. "I will take your rifle
though." He reached out, grabbing it by the stock. At
first he wasn't able to budge it at all. Then I released my
grip, knowing that on my worst day I could take any one
of these birds. Trouble was I had the odds stacked
against me at the moment and one false move might well
mean I'd never finish out this hand. So I let him have
the rifle, but the look on my face never changed. Not
one bit. Not just because I'd been called old, but because this young flannelmouth seemed to have taken
some sort of perverted joy in doing so.

"Shall we proceed to your chuck wagon and your trail
boss, friend?" Lem said. He had the upper hand and
knew it and was playing it for all he could get.

"Sure," I mumbled, my look still concentrated on the
fellow who now had my rifle.

Then we headed for the wagon at a steady pace.

Now, son, I didn't get the nickname Black Jack for
nothing. No man in this land ever got labeled a monicker
without a cause. Nearly every outfit had one man named
Slim, just like ours, and you can believe that the man
was tall and toothpick thin . . . just like our Slim. Me,
I've done a lot of things in my lifetime. Trapped beaver,
worked as a guide, took on any kind of work I could find
that enabled me to stay on that mount of mine. But one
of the best things I'd made my living at wasn't done on a

horse at all. It was done in a seat at a table with a handful of other men playing cards. Black jack and damn near any kind of poker you could think of, not to mention a few that no one had heard of, that's what I was good at. Whether you believe it or not, the games did teach me a couple of things that have come in handy over the years. One of them was patience; waiting is always the hardest part of anything, whether you're playing out a hand at a card table or anticipating a battle. Another thing I'd learned was how to run a bluff; comes in handy when you can carry through with it. And after a while you learn how to spot a cheat who's dealing you seconds.

Lem Cordova—or whatever his name was—would never last in a fair poker game. A carpetbagger is what he was. I'd heard of them but never really had any dealings with them yet. But if old Lem was any example, why, they oughtta hang every one of them, just like I'd heard the Texicans say. Came out of the North, these carpetbaggers did, trying to make the most of the chaos that had apparently spread throughout the South at the end of the war. From what I'd heard, they'd come into your community and falsely represent themselves as some kind of phony businessmen. They'd either buy you or buy you out, one, and take over as much of what was once yours as they could. But their reputation had preceded them when they made it to Texas and that didn't do them any good at all. It's hard enough being on the losing side of a war. But when the other side comes to try to take away your home and what your daddy fought for . . . well, you get mad. These Texas folk weren't having none of the scum they called carpetbaggers. Let's put it this way, if Tom Lang and his boys were there right now, Lem and his boys wouldn't be called carpetbaggers—they'd be called *dead*. Now, hoss, that is hatred.

Lem Cordova wasn't hiding the fact that he was dealing seconds. Me, I'd learned a thing or two about dealing from the bottom of the deck my own self. My mind had been racing faster than the horses and by the time that chuck wagon came into sight on the horizon, I'd determined that this carpetbagger was going to know better. The flannelmouth, well, he might not finish out the day if he kept on pushing.

"Afternoon, Black Jack," Maria said, giving me a quick glance out of the corner of her eye. "I'll set a few extra plates for supper." She seemed in a pleasant mood working at the back of the chuck wagon like she was. What I was counting on in part though was the way men tended to take in her body upon first seeing her. Like I said, we're talking distractions. "Oh," she added with less enthusiasm upon seeing the scraggly bunch that had ridden in with me. I had a notion it wasn't just the men in Texas who had it in for anyone resembling a carpet-bagger.

"Maria, I'm gonna need—" Latch Key froze solid as he rounded the corner of the wagon. "Come in early, did you, Hooker?" He was taking in the lot of them as he spoke, the tone in his voice changing just a mite. Things weren't the way they should have been and he knew it. What was more important, he was letting me know it in his own subtle way.

I shrugged. "Crew ain't far behind." No one had pulled a gun yet, but I do believe we all knew it could happen any second now. Me, I was going to stretch this out as far as I could. "Met these fellas back a ways, cookie. Seems we're crossing their land and they charge a dollar a head." I shrugged again, trying to act harm-less enough. "Figured I'd bring 'em right to the trail boss, him being as free with that money as he is. Pay 'em off and get on with the drive."

That should have been enough to tip Latch Key to how queer this situation was. First off, Tom Lang didn't have much of a say at all as far as the financing of this drive went. That was all Diah's money that was being put up. As for Lang being free with his money, I had a notion it was as hard getting spare coins out of him as it was pulling the back teeth of a she-bear right after her cubs were born. Of course, there was always the matter of my new Winchester, too. Maybe these birds didn't know it, but everyone in camp knew how I felt about having my rifle at my side. Right now all I had in my hands were the reins of my mount. Latch Key nodded.

"Know what you mean, Hooker." To Maria he said, "Darlin', why don't you get one of them empty flour sacks in the wagon and fill it with conscript and some of them coins."

"Well . . . if you say so." Disagreeable is how she looked now.

"You just go ahead and do it, hon."

"And be quick about it, woman!" This last came from the loudmouth who was now situated on the far right of me.

"Watch your mouth, son." Latch Key might have known he was in a dangerous situation, but he wasn't taking any guff from anyone concerning his woman.

"Shut up, Carl," Lem Cordova said before the youngster could go on.

That seemed to do it, for the pushy kid kept silent all the while Maria was inside the wagon. No one spoke, the only sound being the clinky noise made by gold coins. The whole time they were listening to that noise I was trying to figure out how in hell I was going to get out of the fix. It was Latch Key, Maria, and me against these thieves, and I don't mind telling you that I didn't have much faith in the woman, feisty talk or not. What made it even worse was the fact that we had to keep from doing any shooting; hell, we had to keep *them* from doing any shooting! The herd wasn't anywhere close yet, but I wasn't willing to take a chance on starting a stampede. The only thing I knew for sure right then was that two of them were on my right and the rest were on my left. And so far nobody had dismounted or drawn a gun.

"Honey, would you mind giving me a hand?" Maria said as she climbed over the front seat of the wagon and proceeded to back down real careful like. Even mixing that conscript with the gold coin, that flour sack weighed a hefty amount, you bet. Latch Key reached up behind her, his two big hands taking hold of her middle,

fitting easily over the work shirt she wore loose outside
her britches. When she was on the ground she giggled,
an act that got everyone's attention. Then turning to her
husband, she said, "Not now, sugar," and leaned over
to kiss him. What she was leaning over was that flour
bag she held between them with both hands. I reckon
that kiss shocked Latch Key as much as it did the rest of
us, but I was hoping I was the only one who saw what
really went on. Distractions, remember? We're talking
distractions. That Maria, she had a head about her, that
she did.

"I suppose you'll want to count this," she said to
Lem in a sugar sweet voice, her eyes glued to Latch
Key. She moved back to the business end of the chuck
wagon, carrying the sack of money with her. Latch Key
had developed a sudden itch beneath the apron he wore,
but no one seemed to care much, which was fine with
me. They all had their eyes on Maria or the money—or
both.

"Absolutely, my dear." Lem dismounted, trying to
smile as charmingly as he could, which wasn't much. He
took the sack from Maria but not his eyes as he reached
down inside to retrieve a handful of money. I couldn't
see all of his face, but suddenly he sounded like he'd
been bitten by the love bug. Well, son, he got bitten all
right, but it wasn't by the love bug.

"Ow!" he screamed, pulling his hand out of the sack
as though it had been touched by fire. Like I said, those
tarantulas can play hell with your disposition and that
was what he'd just come in contact with. Yes, sir. His
bowler hat fell off and he started to cuss something
fierce, trying to do three things at one time. His curiosity was telling him to take another gander inside that bag
and make sure it actually had some money in it. The
second two things sort of went together I think. He
wanted to pull his six-gun and then beat the living day-
lights out of Maria—or kill her outright. Let me tell you,
son, the only thing he managed to do was to take a look
see inside that sack to find out what it was he was
holding, which sure enough was some of Diah's gold and

conscript. By the time he looked up again, Maria had grabbed hold of an iron skillet from the hinged lid that served as her work table and brought it up alongside his head real hard. I didn't see him hit the ground, but I'd bet all of Diah's money that by the time that hombre did touch the dirt he had a knot on his head that would sweat a rat to run around.

The reason I didn't see old Lem hit the ground was because as soon as Maria hit him, everyone got real busy. Truth to tell, I don't think none of us was sure what it was the others were doing. And that'll rattle you.

But these fellows got even more rattled than I figured. You see, Eagle Feather stepped out from behind that wagon and threw his knife square into the chest of that partner of Lem's. When Lem came to, he was going to find out that he didn't have a partner anymore, not a breathing one at least.

I only heard part of what Latch Key said when he pulled that short-barreled Dragoon out from under that apron, but it had something to do with the buzzards being fed before sunset and the food not coming out of Latch Key's pot. Persuasive, he was.

Me, I backhanded the yahoo on my right, knocking him off his horse. While he was rolling to the ground, I eased out of my saddle right quick and made my way around the back side of his mount to finish him. It wasn't until I was full around the horses rump that I realized I'd likely get shot by his friend the loudmouth.

I didn't.

Oh, the man I'd knocked off the horse was already up on his feet and charging me, his fist connecting with my stomach. Maybe I am getting a might slow. But that flannelmouth was frozen solid, the only thing in his body moving being his eyes. You'd have thought he was a spectator more than one of this gang he was riding with. That was what saved me. But it didn't do a hell of a lot for his partner. While I was falling backwards, you can bet I took a firm hold on his arms and lifted him up and over me with a boost from my feet as I completed a backwards somersault. We both did some scrambling around on the dirt then, him doing his best to try to get his footing again. Me, I grabbed a hank of his hair and pulled him back down to my level. He was pushing himself up when I hit him hard alongside the head and he fell like a rock.

"Sonofabitch," I muttered, rubbing my hand as I got up. Bone on bone hurts like hell. Take my word for it. But the sight I saw made me forget all about it.

It wasn't those two fellows who were still mounted and still had their hands up in the air. Nor the two ringleaders, one of them dead, the other out cold on the ground. Or Eagle Feather standing there at what the army called port arms, his rifle at the ready. What made me forget about the pain was the sight of that flannel-mouth digging his heels into the side of his mount and lighting a shuck. Any other time that might not have mattered, but, my God, he had my Winchester! "Sonofabitch," I said again.

"Watch your mouth, Hooker," Latch Key said, still feeling salty with that pistol in his hand.

"Mister," I said, when I'd grabbed up my reins and climbed back in the saddle, "someone steals my god-damn rifle, I'll talk any way I want!" To Maria I said, "Beggin' your pardon, ma'am. Right handy with a skillet. Yes, ma'am."

Then I dug the heels in my own mount. That boy might have lit a shuck, but I was hell bent on putting out the fire and salting his tail down something fierce. One thing about that old mustang of mine. He's got heart. And he poured it out that next half mile, that he did. All I had to do was follow the dust this lad was leaving behind and I'd find him. The way it was going, it wouldn't be long either. The dust started getting thicker and before you knew it I was right up there alongside him. Got close enough to jump him, sending the both of us down to the fast-moving ground at a thud. Don't ever make a habit of doing that, son, not if you don't have to. If you're young you'll just find out how it sounds when your bones crack as you get older. If you're . . . experienced, like me, well, I reckon you find a few more bones that'll crack next time you move.

"A big mouth don't make a big man," I said as he got to his feet and I hit him.

I don't know if it was the fall from the horse or being hit by me that broke his spirit, but it was broken. Fear was coming to his eyes about the same time his hand was going for his gun. I kicked the gun away from him, sending it bouncing across the dirt and sand. It would need a good cleaning before it could be effectively fired again.

"Smart ass," I growled at him. "Come on, I'm just an *old man*. You oughtta be able to beat the hell outta me."

"Why do I get the feeling you've got a mind to kill that boy?" Tom Lang said when he arrived ten minutes later, having rounded up both of our horses, which had run off during the fight. The loudmouth was still lying there on the ground, figuring it for the safest place to be about now. It may have been the only right decision he'd made all that day.

"Ary you found my rifle, you'd know the answer to that," was my reply.

"I did." When I looked up at him, Lang was smiling at me. He tossed me the Winchester, which would also need a good cleaning before it was fired again. To the youngster, Lang snarled, "Come on, pilgrim, get on your horse." He shook his head slowly as the terrified would-be gunman frantically scurried to his mount, his eyes on me all the time. "Don't seem like any of you young 'uns know how to pick the right profession these days."

"Know what you mean," I said, gathering up my reins.

It was now getting toward the time the herd ought to be circling for the day, so we let the horses have their heads on the way back. The conversation was about as dry as the plains that short trip back, all except for one comment Tom Lang made.

"You know, Hooker," he said, the smile reappearing, "I still ain't so sure about the Juarez boys and the others, but I figure you'll do to ride the river with."

I moved a shoulder around in a circular motion, listened to a couple more bones creak with the movement. I had a feeling Tom Lang heard them, too. Then I wrinkled up those crows feet of mine and gave him a smile, if he could find it through all those whiskers.

"Hell, son, that's what I been tellin' you all along."

Chapter 12

My bones ached like hell when we rode into camp, and I was looking forward to relaxing for a spell, but I'll tell you, son, getting through supper that night got to be a real chore. Yes, sir.

"Matthew, you're so fired up 'bout these weapons, see can you clean this brass boy up," I said, tossing the rifle to him. I hadn't noticed it much before, but every time I'd made reference to my new long gun in front of Matthew, I'd gotten a tad of a smile from him. Reminded me of the kind of grin he used to wear when he tried to pilfer some of his mother's cookies without her knowing. It was the sort of smile that didn't want to come out because it was hiding something.

"You bet, Pa," he said, giving his brother a sidelong glance and that same hint of a smile. Something told me there were things going on that I wasn't aware of. Me, I never was much on surprises.

"Eagle," Lang said, dismounting, "you're a good Injun." What with the Indian wars having flared up again during the War Between the States and showing no signs of letting up even now, most folks on the frontier had taken to the belief that the only good Indian was a dead one. "You done well here when it counted and that sets well in my tally book," Lang continued. Hearing him talk that civil to an Indian seemed an impossibility at best. What really surprised those of us who witnessed it was the trail boss offering his hand to Eagle Feather.

That hand hung out there in midair for longer than you might expect, as the chief likely ran a few tallies of his own through his mind. Finally, he took Tom Lang's hand in friendship.

"I am a good *Ute*," he said, stone-faced, correcting Lang on what he must have thought to be a finer point in his statement.

I had no doubt that there were men walking this land who would easily say what Lang had to an Indian before shooting him in cold blood. Still, I had a notion the two men had come to an understanding that would insure peace between them, at least through the rest of the drive.

"Yeah," Lang agreed. "Sure." Turning his attention to Latch Key, he added, "You too, cookie." One thing about Tom Lang, he gave credit where credit was due. Well, almost.

"What about me, you old Brass Bottom!" Maria said as the Texan walked away. She hadn't been given any credit for her part in this fiasco this afternoon and she sounded madder than hell about it. Not that you could blame her. But if stopping Lang in his tracks was what she had in mind, well, she did it.

"What did you say?" The smile was gone as he turned around and gave her a look that was as crusty as his voice.

"I said what about me, you old Brass Bottom!" Fury was building in her now as she planted her hands on her hips. I had an idea Tom Lang hadn't been talked to like that by any woman but his mother.

"Better watch out, Tom," I said, faking a fearful look. "She's liable to fight you like a man, and you know what that means." The rest of the camp thought the prospect of this woman baring her chest to fight the Texan in a bare knuckle toe-to-toe match was funny, but the two people concerned had lost their sense of humor for right now. Me, I'd just gotten through a bone busting experience and had no desire to get mixed up in another one.

"Oh, shut up, you pompous old bastard!" she threw at me. Testy, she was. "Anyone mentions brass in this camp, I can't tell whether they're talking about his bottom"—here she motioned toward Lang—"or your boy." An over-the-shoulder glance at Diah followed this last. Like I said, I had an idea there was something going on here that I didn't know about. The only comfort I got was seeing the looks of confusion on the faces of Tom Lang and Diah, knowing they were in the same predicament as me.

"Just what are you getting at?" Tom Lang was back to his usual frame of mind. It might have sounded like a question, but you can bet it was a demand that had better be answered.

"Look, mister, I had as much to do with capturing these carpetbaggers this afternoon as any of you. If I hadn't gotten that pistol out to Latch Key, why, it wouldn't have mattered whether the chief planted a knife in that one buzzard or not. If the cookie hadn't had the drop on the two that he did, we'd all be dead right now." Her eyebrows were knit in one hell of a frown. She had been speaking to anyone in camp who cared to listen, but now she directed her harsh words at Tom Lang. "And your precious damn herd would've been scattered to hell and gone."

"Got a point, Thomas," I said cautiously, "that she does."

"All right, lady, you've got my thanks," the Texan said impatiently. "Now, what's this brass bottom stuff?" Slim, Bob, and Charlie were the only three of Lang's crew who were in camp then; Davy and Frank were out watching the herd. Trouble was, Lang's boys, all of them standing behind him now, were getting a mite fidgety, which gave me an idea of what was going on.

"You act tougher than nails, Lang, but they call you old Brass Bottom." Maria was getting it out of her system, all that venom she felt for the boss man.

When Lang turned to face the three hands, he had

only to spot the makings of a smile on one of their faces before deciding what he needed to do. Slim, he was tall and reedy, but he fell like an oak tree when Lang hit him. Just takes the taller ones longer to hit the ground, I reckon. The other two stepped out to each side, in case Lang was figuring on beating their compadre to death.

"Boys," he said, "we're gonna talk. And you're gonna do the listening. Got that?" Another order, followed by nods from the two men still standing. The last I saw, Lang was ushering his men off to one side of the camp for that talk.

"What were you saying about me?" Diah asked, stepping forward.

"Guns, here," Maria said, "calls you the Brass Boy."

Matthew's smile was sheepish when I looked at him. "You said yourself he was a brassy boy." But Diah didn't like it one bit. No, sir.

Maria turned to me. "And you're—"

"I know what I am, sis," I said, poking a finger at her. "Tired and hungry is what I am."

"Look," Latch Key said, trying to come to her aid. Trying was as far as he got.

"Tired and hungry," I repeated to the man. "Your woman's already pushed her luck to the limit. Don't you start on me."

I never did get a chance to hear his reply. There was a grunt and then another one behind me. When I turned, it was Matthew and Diah going at it again, Diah getting the worst of it. I was about to step in and break it up when I heard one of the five prisoners break out in laughter at it all. I'd nearly forgotten about them, but there they were, standing in line on the far side of camp like a squad of soldiers waiting to be inspected. The difference was that these birds had their hands tied behind their backs.

"Haw, haw, haw." Not a regular laugh, this one. More like laughter at another's expense.

I spotted him right off. He was the loudmouth I'd jumped and beaten this afternoon when things got kind of thick. I didn't care for him then, and I damn sure didn't feel that good about him now. It only took a few

strides to reach him and before I even came to a halt I'd
swung a roundhouse punch at him, knocking him flat
against the supply wagon in back of him. He sank to the
ground half conscious.

"If you're trying to get my attention, son, you're
going about it the wrong way," I growled.

His compadres each took an automatic step forward,
the way you do when a friend's in need of help. If my
taking them all on was what they wanted, I'd have
gladly untied them. Didn't have to. That one step was as
far as they dared to go. I had a suspicion I knew why,
hearing what I did to my rear. Of course, they saw it so
it had a greater impact on them, I reckon. Over my
shoulder I'd heard what could have been one or two
guns being cocked, but taking a gander now I saw that it
was all four pistols those Juarez boys carried, ready to
fire. And wouldn't you know it, they were pointed right
at these fellows. Seemed to be a lot of bucking the tiger
going on that day.

"Big mistake," the chief said, shaking his head at
these yahoos.

"*Es verdad,*" Jorge grumbled in that low voice of his.

"We will watch these *hombres*, señor," Bud said.
"You have a family dispute."

"Want to give me a hand?" I asked Long John, who
seemed to be the only one left who wasn't occupied one
way or another.

"No, thanks," he replied a bit sheepishly. "I never
did like getting mixed up in family feuds. I'll just watch
the fire." With that he quickly stepped around the campfire to catch a back-stepping Diah. "See," he added as
my youngest regained his footing and left John's arms to
do battle once more with his big brother. "Somebody's
gotta watch the coffee!"

By then I wasn't going to argue with him. I moved
toward the two battling brothers, knowing just how I'd
break up this fandango. Both had bloodied faces, but it
was Diah who wasn't faring so well at the moment.
Matthew hit him again, sending him sprawling backwards until he fell to the ground, too dazed to get up. As

Diah went down, I continued to march toward his older
brother. Matthew was a big man and there wasn't much
more than pure fury in his eyes now as he glared at
Diah, waiting for him to get up and take more punish-
ment. The intensity in his look worked for me. Oh, he
might have recognized me walking toward him, but he
wasn't ready for what I did. I walked up to him and
stopped right beside him. Then, quick as could be, I had
a hand up around his throat and my near foot behind his,
kicking it out from under him as I leaned into him with
my hip and pushed the upper part of him back until he'd
lost his balance. When that boy falls you can bet the
earth moves, and it ain't got a damn thing to do with
being with a woman.

"Last time I did that was ten years ago," I said to
Matthew, knowing he'd want to know why I'd done it.
"Son, your memory's worse than mine.

"As I recall," I said, turning my attention to Diah,
who was slowly getting to his feet, "it had something
to do with names then, too." I shook my head. "I
do believe that Jed Smith is the only other mountain
man who's ever caused more trouble in my family than
me."

"I don't need you to finish my fights," Diah said.
Defiant? Hoss, that doesn't even come close to how that
boy sounded.

"I'll remember you said that." Me, I was feeling a
mite crusty my own self. "Of course, the next time you
say it will be the last time you do 'cause I'll personally
take the teeth right outta your mouth."

"I'm leaving," Diah said. Now it was his eyes that
blazed, at me, his own father.

"The hell you are, *sonny*," I said in as hard a voice as
I'd ever spoken to the boy. "You haul that carcass of
yours out yonder." I pointed away from the camp. "We
got some talking to do."

"Now you're telling him, Pa," Matthew said with a
crooked smile.

"Oh, he ain't the only one gonna be in on this palaver, son. Soon's you wipe that grin off'n your face you

can join him out there.'' I think that hit him about as hard as my throwing him to the ground had done.

"Show's over, folks," Latch Key said. "Leastwise, iffen you want food it is.'' The mention of food brought back to mind how long the day had been and there was soon a disorganized line formed to get a decent meal before nighthawking began. "Maria, get your medicinals and tend to those Hooker boys," the cook added. "I can handle these mangy critters."

"And bring coffee," I added over my shoulder as I left camp. "Lots of it."

Chapter 13

She brought the coffee first, three steaming cups of it. I don't know how she managed to keep from spilling any, as hot as those cups were, but she did. When she said she'd be back in a minute with her medicines, she might as well have been talking to herself.

We were a ways out from the camp. Not far enough to be out of sight but enough so we wouldn't be heard by anyone wanting to listen in on a family argument.

"Now, *children*, I want to know what it is that's going on."

"Don't talk like that to us, Pa," Matthew said.

"Then stop acting like you're living fifteen years ago instead of today and tell me what's on your minds," I demanded. When neither spoke, I figured I'd throw in my own thoughts first. Maybe that would give them something to work from. "I brought you two together because you hadn't seen one another for some time. I knew this trail drive was going to be a big project and I'd have to have people I could trust with me.

"You wanted to chip in with that money of yours, Diah, and that's fine. I really do appreciate it. Got us a lot more than I ever figured we'd have on hand." I took a gulp of coffee, noticing it was laced with a mite of decent tasting sour mash and set the cup on the ground next to me. That whiskey warmed my innards right quick, but hoss, I still had an ice cold stare on my face for my youngest. I let him know just how much he was bothering me when I drove a fist into the palm of my hand. "But damn it, son, you've been carrying a grudge ever since your brother showed up. Now, I want to know what the hell it's about or you can leave camp, money and all." I think that set him back some, hearing that, for no man really expects his father to give him ultimatums like that when he's a grown, responsible man. But maybe that was it—Jedediah Strong Smith Hooker was full grown but only wanted to be responsible up to a point.

"Your daddy's right, you know," Maria said, setting down an armful of bottles, torn cloth, and bandages next to a small dishpan of water she juggled in the other hand. "Something as big as this cattle drive, why, you're gonna have to set your feelings aside until it's over. We're gonna need every bit of help we can get, Latch Key says."

"You want her around, Pa?" Diah asked, giving her a suspicious glance. After all, it had been Maria who had started it all. I gave her a glance, stroked my chin whiskers, and made up my mind.

"Ary you want to get doctored up, yes." That was what I told them, but the purpose I had in mind was a tad different. The two gave me cautious looks but knew better than to sass me in my present mood. "Go ahead, son. Maria, here, she ain't gonna tell no one 'bout this palaver." I cocked an eye directly at her, giving it a mite of a squint as I added, *"Are you?"* One way or another she was going to know I meant business.

"Why, no, of course not," she gulped nervously. Then she set about to fixing up their faces.

"I'm waiting," I said when Diah didn't say anything for a bit.

"It's that name. Jed Smith." Frustrated is what the boy was. He didn't want to talk about it if the expression on his face was any gauge.

"What about it?"

"It's just the name," he shrugged. "You name me

after some mountain man you knew and then you spend
the whole of my life doing what you think is funning."
Fire came back to his eyes as he gave a hateful glance at
his brother. "*Both* of you," he spit out, and I saw some
blood fly out with the words.

He coughed some, turning to the side to spit out more
blood. While he did I gave Matthew a silent, hard glare
of my own along with a shake of the head, hoping he
had the brains to pick up on what I was hinting at. If he
didn't, the woman did.

"You know, Guns," she said, dabbing at his cheek,
"you really ought to *lay off* the hard stuff." Maybe it
was the way she said it right into his ear that brought
him around.

"So I've been told."

When Diah turned back to us, he was, no less, madder
than before.

"Pushy, that's what you've been," he said. "Both of
you. You think it's some kind of game, but it's pushy.

"Why the hell should I have to measure myself up
against someone else, Pa?" he exploded. "Why?" The
furrow that had grown in his forehead could have been
put there by a Missouri mule, but all of a sudden he
sounded like he could have cried. Somehow or other we
had hurt him bad. Mind you, I could chalk it up to the
lad having his mother's sensitive side, which was true,
but this was strictly between the four of us; the three
Hookers and a mountain man named Jedediah Strong
Smith.

"Well, I won't take it anymore," Diah said.

A smile came to Matthew's bloodied face. "See, Pa,
told you he was a brassy boy." He seemed intent on
having at it again with Diah.

"Now, you stop it right there, *sonny*," I said, hard
and mean. If he thought he was being talked to like
some ten-year-old, so much the better for that was exactly what I was doing. "For your information and
eddication, the only brass boys in this camp are our
Winchesters." Matthew got the idea. But the fire wasn't
gone from Diah, not by any means.

"You want to know if I've done something *heroic* lately? Want to know if I've done anything to rival your Jed Smith? Well, yes, as a matter of fact I did, Pa." He could have been one of those hellfire and brimstone circuit riders you run across every once in a while, as much forcefulness as he had in him now. Right along with a mixture of fear and pain.

"You remember how I told you your friend Samuel Botkin died, Pa?"

"Sure. You said he went after the bunch that killed his daughter. What was her name? Rebecca?"

"That's right." The fire had died in him, the voice softening. It was pain he was talking about now, pain he was feeling as he spoke. I know because I've been through it my own self. "But I called her Becky and she was the most beautiful woman who ever lived. You see, I loved her. We were going to get married."

"Oh, my God," Maria said, drawing it out slowly, knowing in her mind, just like Matthew and I did, what he must have gone through.

"It wasn't just Samuel that went after 'em, Pa. I was right there beside him when we hunted 'em down."

He went back to the start of it then, which was the only part of the story that I knew all that well. Samuel Botkin had been a good friend of mine. When he asked my recommendation for someone to help escort his daughter out from back east to Denver, I told him Diah was a good choice. Diah had agreed to take on the job. Other than that he had only mentioned to me that Samuel had been killed avenging the death of his daughter. But sitting there and listening to him, well, I reckon there was a lot that had gone on that he hadn't told me. And as he spoke I got the notion that there were some things that had happened he never would tell anyone.

I'd heard about Chivington, of course, and the bloody Colorado Third and the Sand Creek Massacre back in '64, but I had no idea that my own boy had been there. There was also a lot of hatred and fear of Indians going on in Denver at the time. Samuel's wife had been Mexican, I knew. Oddly enough, that was what got Rebecca

Botkin killed. It seems that most everyone in Denver figured her for a half breed, and indeed she was, except that the Denver folks figured her other half was Indian instead of Mexican. She and Diah had fallen in love and planned to be married late in the fall. It was just after Sand Creek that Diah returned to Denver to find his Becky strung up in a storefront window. An "example" is how the good townfolk tried explaining it. He found Samuel, who'd been beaten within an inch of his own life, then located the men who'd done the killing. They weren't any farther than the edge of town, a drunken mob of half a dozen or so. Samuel had died just like Diah said, avenging his daughter's death. But it was Diah and the town marshal who had given most of those culprits a one-way ticket to hell. The marshal had died, too, and Diah damn near.

"Yeah, I did something heroic," he added when he'd finished his story. "Live up to your Jed Smith's standards, does it?"

"You hush now, Diah," Maria said, moving her medicinals from Matthew to his brother. She'd fixed up Matthew's face in short order, then listened to Diah's story with as much interest as the rest of us as he spun it out. The tragedy had touched her as much as it had Matthew and I. She sniffled some as she said, "Can't have you talking the same time I fix you up." I had a notion it was more her not wanting to hear any more of what he had to say.

Diah's story had pretty much shut his brother's mouth; Matthew couldn't find anything funny to josh his brother about anymore. Of course, my eldest wasn't the kind to apologize for much of anything either, so after a long silence I did my best to make things right again—if that was possible.

"You know, son, one of the things I always admired 'bout Jed Smith was the fact that he was different from most other mountain men. 'Twasn't the bravery either. No, sir. I reckon it was the privacy the man held about what he did. Didn't brag like others would. Quiet man, he was, kept to himself a lot like you've been doing. Ary he had pain or troubles, well, I reckon he kept that to himself, too. Whichever it was, it never did show in how he did his work . . . or anything else.'' I paused, trying to think of more words, better words to say, but there weren't any. "Maybe that's how the man was measured in his day. I know that's how most of us saw him.''

I chuckled, remembering him.

"A mite like your mother, he was. Put his faith in the Good Book. Long as he had that, his rifle, and the clothes on his back, why, he figured he could go any-where and do anything. Maybe that's hard for you to understand, but let me tell you, son, when I was first starting out way back when, they had a saying that God seldom ventured to the west of the Missouri River. Me, I've been around long enough to know that there's much more than a handful of truth in that, which is why I tend to chuckle at a man putting all his faith in the Good Book. Jed Smith took that rifle and his Bible; me, I took my rifle and *more powder and ball*. That's what's kept me alive.

"But the three of us are family, Diah,'' I said in earnest. "Or what's left of it,'' I added, remembering Martha who was now long dead. "We don't pull to-gether, we likely ain't worth much more'n the spit and sawdust we're made of. As for your Becky—''

"Ain't nothing we can do except tell you how sorry we are,'' Matthew said to my surprise, for they were nearly the same words I had in mind. "You done more'n I've ever heard Pa say was done by Smith. I won't josh you again about that name.''

"Isn't that sweet,'' Maria said, sounding happy again. Diah and I were staring at one another in shock at Matthew's words.

She was done patching up Diah after a minute that was filled with nothing but silence. Either the well had gone dry of words or none of the four of us were feeling chancy enough to start up another conversation, one. Then I remembered we had other things to do, like eat.

"Maria, how 'bout you see can you find us some plates with food on 'em. Matthew, give her a hand with these bandages and such." Neither of them spoke but went about doing as I said. Just before the woman left I thought I caught something in her eye, and when she gave me a full glance, I knew we had sparked something in her. She'd heard us Hookers talking and that had her thinking, which is just what I wanted if what I suspicioned proved right.

"That Becky, she was special to you, wasn't she, son?" I said when Diah and I got to our feet. It was just the two of us and there was a purpose for that, too.

"Yeah, Pa, she was." He said it sadly and I knew the memory was a bittersweet one.

"Scars inside you take longer to heal than the ones you can see." Did you ever say something and then feel like you were just talking for your own sake? Hell, the boy likely already knew what I was saying, all of which made me feel a mite stupid for speaking the words. Still, there was something he had to know, something that I could only say to him alone.

"When I told you that Jed Smith was different from the rest of us . . . well, he was. He made his own trails and was his own man. Maybe I looked too much for that in you. But you've got to know, son, that you're just as special to me as your Becky was to you."

"That just come to you, did it?" The boy was still mad, still bitter, but at least I now knew why. If anyone else had spoken to me in the tone of voice Diah had just used, I would have bloodied his lip and broken his jaw. Instead I swallowed hard and looked him square in the eye.

"Matter of fact, it goes all the way back to the first day you sassed me." He wasn't expecting it, wasn't quite sure of what I'd said or why, and his expression showed it. I reckon love in a family comes hard sometimes, but it's not the kind you forget easy. Diah, he wasn't about to forget my words any too soon. I raised a bushy eyebrow, gave him a sidelong glance as though he were some stranger I was about to tangle with. *"The day you were born, son, it was the day you were born.''*

He had a look of disbelief about him when I left to get that plate of food and some more coffee.

Like I said, it was one hell of a long day.

Chapter 14

Tom Lang must have straightened his boys out, too, for it was awful quiet after supper that night. Or maybe it was having those prisoners in camp. Whatever it was, things finally got back to normal the next morning.

Almost.

"Guns, Diah, you two are gonna be eating dust today," the Texan said as we wolfed down breakfast. It wasn't anything my boys figured on hearing, which likely accounted for whatever they had in their mouths going down the wrong way as Lang spoke.

"What!" came the hoarse reply from each.

"You know the camp rules," Lang said. "They include no fighting. And you'd have one helluva time convincing me what you two were doing yesterday was showing brotherly love. Besides," he added with that galling twist of the mouth he called a smile, "I'm the boss." Normally, my boys would've challenged him, but when he nodded in my direction and added, "And he suggested it," they did nothing more than give me glaring looks.

"And what position do we take up, señor?" Bud asked. It was the Juarez boys, you recall, who had been put on permanent drag. To say that the expression on their faces now was one of relief would be putting it mildly.

"Nothing on my drive, boys," Lang replied. "I can fill in Guns' position on the flank, but you two are gonna help Black Jack get the prisoners to a town just east of here. Two Dog is what it's called, if I recollect right. Even got a jail with bars I hear." To Latch Key he said, "Cookie, if you got your list of supplies ready, you can pick 'em up there, too.

"Come on, you loafers," he said to the rest of the outfit, gulping down the remains of his coffee, "we've got a herd to move."

Latch Key and Maria broke camp while he got the herd strung out, the Juarez lads keeping an eye on our unwelcome strangers. But when I got back to camp, the first thing I saw was Latch Key giving the list he'd made up to the woman.

"Wait just a minute here, people," I said, barging right in on their conversation. Not that I like being impolite, you understand, but I knew exactly what Lang was talking about when he reminded the crew each morning that they were burning daylight. Time to spare was something a body never had much of on a cattle drive. "You ain't thinkin' of sendin' *her*, are you?" I asked in pure contempt.

"Hell, yes," the cook replied. "She's at least got someone to look after her if she goes along with you three. If I send her ahead by her lonesome, why, there's no telling what'll happen to her." Throwing a hateful glance at our prisoners, he added, "Especially if they's more of these varmints out there."

"I don't like it, cookie," I said, but it wasn't him I was talking to when I said it. I was staring straight at Maria. "I'm beginning to believe what Lang said about a woman being bad luck on one of these drives." Hearing that gave her the urge to spout off, but Latch Key beat her to it.

"Look, Hooker, I've been taking care of myself longer than I can remember," he growled. "I just ain't about to take the responsibility for someone else getting killed."

He was looking at Maria all right, but there was something in the way he looked at her, the way he said what he just did, that nudged something in my memory. That little nudge was the only reason I gave in to letting her come along.

She looked madder than hell sitting on top of that supply wagon as we left. Me, I was going to make it work for me. Like I said, I never was too keen on not knowing all of what was going on around me. Having gotten a handle on my boys, I figured it was about time to get a few questions answered about some of the other people on this drive.

According to Lang, it was only a two-hour ride to Two Dog, which meant we could get into town, deposit these tied-up yahoos in the city jail, get the supplies, and even have time enough for a drink before getting back to the drive. *If* these supposed gunmen didn't give us any trouble. But the Juarez fellas read a chapter from the book to the yahoos as they mounted up, in case they had any doubts.

"Señors," Bud addressed them with a smile, "it *es mucho* hard to ride with your hands tied behind your back, but you will do it, so I advise caution."

Jorge wasn't so lighthearted about the matter.

"Es verdad," he grumbled in that deep voice of his. "*Es nada,* nothing, you could do if you left your horse. You couldn't outrun us and if you slip"—here his face twisted up into what could only be described as an imagined horror—"your *caballo,* your horse, could drag you." He grimaced again. "It is an ugly, painful way to die, *mis amigos.*"

That took the wind out of them as much as being kicked in their elsewheres, for they knew Bud and Jorge meant business when it came to death. But then, I reckon dealing in lead and death go hand in hand, if you get my drift.

I didn't think the Juarez boys would have any trouble with our prisoners, and we couldn't go any faster than the supply wagon, so I dropped back alongside the wagon after a bit. Maria still had that contemptuous look on her face and wasn't about to start up a friendly conversation. But the mad she was feeling concerned her pride more than anything else and that was something that seemed to get hurt every day or so now. In this case I was going to make it work for me.

"How come you never got married?" I asked out of the blue. Any other time she might have paid more attention to it, but it was her pride she was all consumed with now and that meant everything else was an automatic answer.

"Hell," she growled, "no one could ever stand up to—" By then she realized the mistake she'd made, and had a stunned expression on her face as she looked my way.

"Don't stop now, darlin'," I said with a smile. "I want to hear it all."

"No one could ever stand up to my brothers or my pa. No one could ever beat 'em in a fight." It wasn't even close to midmorning and she was breaking out in a cold sweat. She wasn't the gal she'd claimed to be, which wasn't all that unusual when you consider how much of it was going around these days. What brought on that cold sweat was her knowing I'd found out something about her secret, something about who she really was.

"Why don't you rein in this wagon a minute, Maria. Let me tie up this mount and move your git up end to the other side of the seat. We never did have a chance to talk an awful lot."

And that we did for the next few miles or so. Maria, she turned out to be an interesting woman. I reckon life does get hard for a woman when you grow up surrounded only by men. You can get to hating that type of animal. Turns out that was what had happened to Maria, or so she said. She ran away one day and told herself she'd never go back. When neither her pa nor her brothers came after her, well, she was stuck out there in the middle of nowhere.

Don't get me wrong now, son, for women can be as tough as men in this land. But it's that first time you meet the challenge that's the hardest, and Maria, well, she wasn't up to it. But then, no one is when they're about to pass out for lack of water and food. Trouble was, the fellow who came upon her wasn't all that well intentioned, if you know what I mean. Had his way with her more than once. Beat her and did any thing he wanted to with her. By the time she recovered, she found out he had plans to put her in some madam's house, which explained what I thought I'd seen in her eyes from the start. Odd part was that now she was taking an actual liking to Latch Key. Yes, sir, Maria was real interesting. But not quite as interesting as Jared Watts.

Two Dog wasn't any different than many another little town that had sprung up along these new trails being forged north. My own pa had a way of looking at life from the money end of it, which is what the folks in these towns were doing, especially if they were brand new. "Find a need and fill it, son." That's what Pa told me when I was a youngster; it's one of the reasons I took to the mountains when those beaver hats came to be the rage. It's what these folks were doing with the cattle drives. Every so often along the thousand mile trail we were traveling, the cook would need to be resupplied. Mind you, there was a time when all a man would need to go into the wilderness was a decent supply of powder and ball, his rifle, a knife and/or ax, and a tad of salt to give his meat flavor when he cooked it. But folks were getting "civilized" and had to have more of the comforts of life, even on the trail. The cook had to have a bit of sugar and flour and a few condiments along with that staple of salt. That was all on Maria's list of supplies, along with one other item she hadn't written down but had told me about. Like I said, we had an interesting talk.

Tom Lang was right about the jail having bars. It was one of those thick-walled adobe structures that stood out in a town that likely had every bit of wood in the area built into its buildings. The jail was near the center of town, right across from the general store, which seemed pretty handy considering that those were the two main stops we had to make. Not that any of us would have worked up a sweat walking from one end of the town to another. It's sort of hard to do when each side of the main street—hell, the only street—had all of eight or nine buildings to it, and at least one or two of them were saloons. No school, no church, no women, no kids in sight. And if this town had got its monicker from a couple of dogs, well, they weren't there anymore either.

"Heat this place up and it would remind me of hell," Maria said as we rode in.

"It is a mite frayed on the edges, ain't it?" I said.

You'd have thought her wearing that oversized buckskin jacket of Latch Key's would have kept these yahoos from leering at her, but every man jack of them on that street was looking at her as though she were as naked as a newborn . . . or wishing it real hard.

"My lord! At last another woman to talk to." There was as much relief in the voice of the woman who appeared in the door of the general store as there had been in the Juarez boys' faces that morning when they were taken off drag duty. I reckon you'd call her middle-aged. When they said this land was hell on women, they weren't joshing. Young or worn out was getting to be the normal choice of descriptions for a woman found in this land. This one was thirty, thirty-five, somewhere around Matthew's age I'd gauge. Perky, though. The flowery dress sort of fit the smile on her face. It half surprised me that I didn't see a youngster in tow behind her.

"God Almighty!" Maria was just as surprised as the other woman.

"I reckon you ladies got other things to talk 'bout now that you've gotten past the Maker," I said half in jest. "Just don't get too longwinded, young lady," I added to Maria. "We still gotta git back to camp."

"I won't," she promised. Me, I knew better. Trying to keep two women from gabbing away at one another is the equivalent of trying to keep a couple of old mountain men from swapping lies. Believe me, son, I know.

"Why don't you boys give these ladies a hand loading

our supplies," I said to Bud and Jorge when the women had disappeared inside. "I'm taking these birds to jail and see can I set up accommodations for 'em. Then I'm going to see how homemade the brew in this place is."

"But—" The two Mexicans were as thirsty as I was and I knew it.

"Hoss, the way I figure it, we could take shifts trying to dry out that saloon and never make a dent in the palavering those females will be doing. Don't you fret, I'll be back to spell you."

That brought smiles to their faces as they set about preparing the wagon for loading and I herded Lem Cordova and what was left of his gang to the jail house. If it had been Latch Key or any other man in the outfit in that store I wouldn't have bothered with having someone keep watch over them. But Maria was turning into a real informative person after that talk we'd had. Besides, she had proven to be a better than average cook.

"Looks like you could use some business," I said to the lawman inside the adobe building. There were three cells in the jail, none of them occupied.

"By the looks of it you're fixing to give me a fair amount." It didn't take more than one glance at the men I'd brought with me to see that they'd lost a lot of their freedom; having your hands tied behind your back will do that to you. "Gar Tucker," the lawman said, offering a hand.

"Black Jack Hooker," I said, taking it. "Passing through. Figured I'd drop off some dead weight." Then I explained what had happened with Cordova and his men.

The marshal nodded. "I've heard of these men but never did see 'em close up. Pushy bunch if the stories are right. Don't you worry, Mister Hooker, we've got ways of taking care of carpetbaggers like these." The lawman didn't like these pilgrims any more than I did.

"Suits me. Long as you keep 'em away from me and mine."

He made fast work of putting them behind bars, letting me know that a circuit judge would be due in a month or two if anyone from my outfit could stop by to testify. "Or I can take a deposition from you if you've a mind."

That suited me fine so I told him I'd write up what he wanted while I had a beer.

The saloon was about as anonymous as the beer they served. I thought the management might have been a mite reluctant to put a name to either one for reasons of its own. Dingy as the back side of some liveries I'd been in, it was. Near smelled as bad, too. Or maybe that was the clientele. What they called beer was homemade all right but tasted little like the real stuff. I wrote out the paper the marshal had asked for and left half of the beer in the glass.

"Ary they got a cantina in this false front they call a town, I'd find it, lads," I said when I relieved Bud and Jorge a short time later. "What they serve for beer in that saloon tastes more like it's been through a panther's liver than any kind of brew I ever came across."

The wagon was close to being fully loaded when I took a seat on the chair out front of the general store, the women still chattering away inside. What they seemed to be doing was picking out one item on the list and doing a bunch of gabbing before they moved on to another item. Likely they changed subjects that way, too. I couldn't hear much of what they were saying but didn't care to either. As long as we didn't take too long to get back to camp.

"Black Jack, we've got some flour back here if you'd give me a hand with it," Maria said, sticking her head out the door.

"Surely, ma'am," I said, tipped my hat and leaned my rifle up against the door jam before following the other lady to the back room to get the supplies. Maria took my place in the chair.

A couple of hefty sacks of flour were what I had to contend with, but I'd tossed around beaver pelts heavier than those sacks and thought nothing of it. I was setting them down toward the back of the wagon when I realized the reason I hadn't thought much about such a chore way back when was because . . . well, it was way back when. But I didn't get much of a chance to ponder it all that much because just then all hell broke loose!

Like I said, there seemed to be a lot of that going around of late.

Chapter 15

Shots rang out inside the jail. No sooner did the ricochet of sound die down than Cordova and his compadres came storming out the jail house door, each carrying at least one pistol or long gun with him. They were quick to mount the nearest horses, giving me short glances as they did so.

"Give me—" I started to yell at Maria, but she'd beat me to it. The fancified lady wisely had disappeared back behind the door, but not Maria. She was turning into a real fire-eater, by God!

"Get down!" she yelled, grabbing up my Brass Boy in the same instant. The escaped prisoners hadn't gotten much past mounting up. Just then the lawman, his chest covered with blood, staggered out to the doorway. If he wasn't dead, he damn sure would be before the sun set. His body was simply going through the motions now; the things a dedicated man would do even in his dying moments. The six-gun in his hand was as red as his chest and bringing it up he looked slow, awful slow. Two more gunshots from the outlaws sealed his fate and he was dead before he hit the ground. But their guns weren't the only ones that fired. My Brass Boy went off and one of them slumped forward in his saddle as Maria levered another round into the Winchester. That second round left another man hatless.

Got their attention real good, she did. Hell's fire, the whole lot of them began throwing lead in our direction, all except the one Maria had shot. A couple of those shots pretty well busted up the plate glass window of the general store. A third one somehow turned into a ricochet, which quickly died out. Where that fourth one got planted, well, hoss, it made me mad.

"Sonofabitch!" I said in no uncertain terms, making sure the rest of the world knew how I felt.

"I beg your pardon!" The lady store owner stuck her head out around the door, her face red as could be.

"Lady," I growled, "that stuff is *heavy*." I directed a quick glance at a stream of flour pouring out into the tailgate of the wagon. It was that bottom flour sack that had taken the fourth bullet, and the weight of the sack atop it wasn't helping to keep any of the flour in.

"Gimme that thing," I added, snatching away the Brass Boy from Maria as she sank back into the chair, her face pale as could be.

Damn it, they were getting away! But there was a lot of *almost* going around the day, and *almost* got away seemed to fit the bill more accurately. The four healthy ones had turned tail to light a shuck out of town while they still had their hair, the wounded one cutting down a back alley with the same thing in mind. They would have gotten away too; trouble was they had picked the wrong direction to leave town in.

Bud and Jorge must have found that cantina I had suggested. Wouldn't you know, it was at the far end of town, the same end these *hombres* were fixing to vamoose from. Two of them never made it. They, along with the rest of us, I reckon, had forgotten about the Juarez boys being a part of our group. Fact is, these outlaws were so busy looking over their shoulders at me and my Winchester that by the time they were on Bud and Jorge, why, they were gone beaver. The Mexicans didn't have any hearing problems a-tall and had planted themselves at the end of the street when the shooting started. Both men had both guns out, shooting from the hip as they planted two slugs each in the front two riders, then moved out of the way as the horses passed them and the dead men fell off. You'd have thought it was some kind of stage play, or something right out of one of those dime novels that they hawked back east. These Juarez boys weren't worth spit in the eyes of Tom Lang, but that point of view was going to change one hell of a lot once we got back to camp, of that I was sure.

It was Lem Cordova who got away. His one lone companion was bouncing up and down so much in his saddle that I wasn't sure what I'd hit when I fired at him. Oddly enough I sent his hat a-flying when I pulled the trigger. Stranger yet, the man pulled in his reins and halted his horse as soon as he lost that headgear! When he threw his hands up I knew it wasn't out of any fear of me shooting at him again. It was looking down the business ends of those Remingtons the Juarez lads had trained on him. Facing those kind of odds will make a man either buck the tiger or throw in his hand. Bucking the tiger you don't always win; throwing in your hand . . . well, at least you usually live long enough to tell about it.

"What in the hell happened to you!" I said, taking in Maria sitting in that chair.

"I don't know, but it's blood and I think it's *my* blood," she said, woefully looking down at her left foot. A hole in the side of the boot was leaking blood. If you were to put money on it, I'd bet it was Maria's foot that had caught that ricochet. It is purely amazing how a body can go from being fearsome to scared to death like Maria had; but then, seeing your own blood is likely to do it to you quicker than anything.

"I have a bed in the back," the lady in the store said when she saw Maria's boot. "If you can get her back there and get that boot off, I'll get a doctor."

I barely got "Yes, ma'am" out of my mouth before she was gone, working her way down the boardwalk, managing her skirts and giving off a cute little sway as she did. Half of the town's population had appeared on the streets just before the gunfire had died down, rifle and pistol in hand. The other half, well, I reckon they were either hunting up their guns or hiding. Those that were out got a look at the lady making her way down the street.

"Hold this," I said, handing Maria the Brass Boy and picking her up in my arms. She had one arm around my neck as I tried to maneuver my way through the store to the back, careful not to hit her foot. Halfway back I nearly dropped her. Not that she was all that heavy, you understand, for she wasn't. It was the surprise I felt when all of a sudden she was half pulling my face down and hers up and kissing me. The whole thing took me by surprise for in all truth I'd have to admit that I hadn't been kissed like that in one hell of a long time. Right tasty, she was.

"Thanks for saving my life, Black Jack." She smiled as she said it, looking like she was enjoying it all even with her foot carrying a piece of lead like it was. Me, I was purely obfusticated about the whole thing. Yes, sir, that's the word for it.

"Horse apples!" was my reply. "Looking out for each other is what we were doing. Besides, you're a damn good shot." I meant it, too.

"I know," she said, smiling. "That's the only thing I ever bested my three brothers at. Shooting." Maria, she was full of surprises that day.

By the time I'd gotten the boot off, the town doctor had arrived. I paid the woman for our supplies and gave the doctor his fee as well, knowing that no matter what the rest of the town was like, he, at least, was one man I could trust to do his best. More than likely he was the only one like that left in Two Dog. Gar Tucker, the marshal, had been the only other one I'd seen who could measure up in this so-called community, and the only thing left of him was a memory. I mentioned to the store owner and the doctor that I wanted to know when Maria was going to be ready to travel. Me, I had some unfinished business to take care of across the street.

"Good day for the carpenter and the undertaker," I said as I walked into the jail house. The Juarez boys had beaten me to getting the lone gang member—or at least the one we still had—back behind bars.

"In this village they will be one and the same," Bud said with a smile.

"*Es verdad.*" His brother seemed to second the motion on damn near everything Bud said.

A young man in his twenties who smelled of the livery stables was standing in the corner, a look of awe about him as he stared at the dead lawman's body.

"Who's he?" I asked.

"The deputy. The part-time man who never thinks he must do his job. *Muy* scared, this one." Bud shook his head in despair. "But we help him, Jorge and I." The grin reappeared and he turned his gaze to his brother.

Help is what they were giving the lad all right. Hell, they were doing his job for him! Jorge was squatting next to the wall facing the cell in which our lone prisoner was nervously seated in a far corner. My shot must have grazed him for he had a small amount of blood trickling down the side of his forehead. But that trickle was the last of his worries by far. Just as the part-time deputy stood in fear and awe of the dead marshal, our prisoner had an equal obsession with the shotgun Jorge Juarez was carefully positioning, its barrel pointed dead center at the prisoner's cell. The whole contraption was rigged so that the slightest movement of the cell door would trigger the scatter gun into action. A man with his wits about him would think of a way to undo it after a while, but the fellow in that cell was about as overcautious as a gopher at a rattlesnake convention. After what he'd been through, he was getting right gun shy. Yes, sir.

"When you feed him, señor," Jorge said to the town's new lawman, "do it from a distance. *Carefully*."

"Give that to your circuit judge when he comes through," I told the frightened stable hand as I handed him the deposition I'd written up for Marshal Tucker. The paper had a drop or two of blood on it from where I'd left it next to Maria's chair across the street. But next to the bloody mess on the lawman's desk and the trail of blood leading to the front door, that was small indeed. "I got a suspicion he ain't gonna need it ary you tell him 'bout how the marshal died," I added sadly, taking one last painful look at Gar Tucker.

"No, sir," the man finally said, speaking for the first time since I'd arrived. "No, sir, not at all."

The bullet in Maria's foot had torn up some of the insides from what the doctor told us. She'd need to stay off her feet for some time before that left foot would be of any use to her again. She had a grim smile on her face as I carried her out to the wagon. There would be no easy way to get her back to the camp in that jouncing wagon but she insisted on going, claiming that was where she belonged. A gamey young lady, this one.

We were late getting back to camp that night. Tom Lang started in to cussing up a storm when we got within hearing range, but quieted down once he saw Maria's foot. To my surprise, Latch Key showed more concern than I figured him for, fussing over Maria like she really was his wife.

Another thing changed before the sun set that night. Tom Lang gained a whole new respect for the Juarez boys when he found out what they'd done. You might say they got initiated into the rest of the crew as being worthy cowhands. Every one of Lang's men knew that these Mexican lads would fight for the brand when the chips were down. And, by God, that meant something to those boys.

Starting the next morning, the position of drag rider was rotated between almost everyone instead of just Bud, Jorge, and my boys.

Hell, even Tom Lang's crew pulled it!

Chapter 16

We weren't the first or the only ones pushing long-horns north to make a profit that year. The Shawnee Trail we were on started out about the same place Jesse Chisholm's did, down on the Rio Grande. Fact of the matter is that until you got up past San Antonio and Austin, why, the two trails were one and the same. Just west of Waco they separated, taking their own directions, the Chisholm Trail passing by Fort Worth while our Shawnee Trail passed by Dallas. Every once in a while there would be a new herd that would join this massive movement north, although each trail boss generally had enough common sense to keep his distance from the others. That was one of the things Eagle Feather was doing out in front of us, keeping Lang and me appraised of how much distance there was between us and the herd ahead of us. Most of the time on that drive we had plenty of elbow room.

Crossing the rivers could be treacherous if it wasn't handled right. If those mangy longhorns got to smelling water, they might stampede toward it and kill themselves in the process, being trampled by those that followed. The Colorado River ran through Austin, the Brazos just north of Waco, and the Red River up around Preston. In between we seemed to find enough creeks and water holes to keep both the herd and the men going.

Some days it seemed like we'd never find any water, but we did.

Now, hoss, depending on who you listen to, that Red River is or isn't the border between Texas and the Indian Territory. So far we'd only had one encounter with the Comanche and they had come in peace to ask for a few head of cattle. I think that surprised the hell out of all of us, so Lang cut a couple of the healthier cattle out to give them along with the usual strays and stragglers from the drag end of the herd. Surprisingly, that satisfied them and we never saw a Comanche again.

It was after we crossed the Canadian River in the Indian Territory that our whole operation slowed down for the better part of one day. If anyone was carrying along one of those fancy calendars, I sure didn't know about it. But I'd been living without one long enough to gauge that we were somewhere in the second month of the drive.

It all started when damn near every one of the crew, me included, got a tremendous urge to make a donation to whatever foliage Mother Nature had in the area right after breakfast that morning. Got to help the earth reproduce, you know. Wasn't none of us looking too awful fit when we climbed back in our saddles either.

"What did cookie put in that coffee this morning, alkali?" Lang asked, seeing the less than adequate performance his crew was giving him.

"That or he found him some bad meat," I said. "You keep 'em going while I go check on it with him."

Latch Key hadn't broken camp yet when I arrived. Maria had only been good for sit-down chores since Two Dog and was just now feeling game enough to take a step or two with that foot of hers. Mostly it was Latch Key who carried her in his arms from here to there to help him out. I also thought I'd seen them give one another glances. Not the kind a married couple will, but the kind that two people who want to get to know one another better but ain't got the courage to take the first step will. It was that kind of look.

"Just what did you put in that mud you call coffee, hoss?" I asked Latch Key in none too jovial a manner.

"No more'n the usual." There wasn't a cook on any of these drives who didn't get a hard time from his men about the food. Complaining about the grub was as close as the crew would come some days to blowing off the steam they'd built up during the course of a day's events. But I was lodging a formal complaint with no funning attached to it and that put Latch Key on the defensive. The stormy look that came to his face now said so.

"Oh, my God!" Maria said, hobbling around the side of the wagon. "You didn't do—" It was her emotions taking over now as she caught herself short. "I mean, you—"

"What the hell's the matter with you people!" Latch Key flared up. "Complain when I fix the damn stuff and complain when I don't. There ain't nothing wrong with my coffee, absolutely *nothing*!" In anger he grabbed a spare tin cup and poured in a slosh of what must have been the last of this morning's brew. A quick sip of the scalding liquid was all he needed to roll around on his tongue before violently spitting it out and turning a mite red in the face. "What in the hell is this!!"

Now, hoss, drinking the last of one of those big pots of coffee is enough to wake any man up, I don't care if his blood is running hot or cold. The six-shooter coffee that was made on the trail was mighty strong, enough so you could have one cup and count on it seeing you through until the next meal, it was that thick. But if you get the dregs of that coffee pot, why, you not only had your fill of hot liquid for the day but solids as well if you swallowed some of those grounds. The way our cook was spitting out his own brew though, you'd have thought it was poison. The same thought was running through Maria's mind I reckon.

"My God, you *poisoned* 'em!" she said in a forceful but hushed voice, her eyes about to fall out of their sockets.

"The hell I did!" He tossed out the contents of the cup, and handed it to the woman. "I'll tell you what,

I'm getting rid of whatever's in this bellywash." As he spoke he took the lid from the huge coffee pot sitting on the burned down logs. He glanced at the contents as he readied to put out the fire with the dregs. But it wasn't until his arm was cocked, ready to toss the coffee, that a surprised look came to his face and he froze solid. Slowly, the pot came down until it was positioned in front of his face again, a look of disbelief still upon his features as he took a second gander inside the pot.

"Jesus, Mary, and Joseph." This time his voice was one notch above a whisper.

Maria took a cautious peek inside the pot, made a squeamish face, and shuddered as she backed away. Couldn't say as I blamed her either.

"Vinegaroons," I muttered, seeing the contents. "No wonder."

The vinegaroon is another variation of the scorpion in the Southwest. Shake your boots out in the morning and one of these critters will leave a hell of an odor while he lights a shuck. Bad as breaking wind, I reckon. Just imagine what would come out of a handful of these pesky things when they got into something like your coffee and got boiled good and hot. There wasn't much life left in the half dozen or so that squirmed around in the used grounds. There was also little doubt in our minds about what had made the men sick this morning either.

"Must've crawled into one of my sacks of Arbuckles," was all Latch Key could say in his astonished voice. But his concern for what he'd given the men was soon over-ridden by his pride as a cook. No man wants to have a mistake shoved down his throat and Latch Key was no different. "Look, Hooker—"

"Never was much for stretching the truth, Latch Key," I said in an even tone, swiping a biscuit from the tail gate of his chuck wagon before picking up my reins. "Boys ask me what got 'em sick, I'm a-gonna tell 'em exactly what it was."

When Latch Key heard that, you just knew he thought his reputation as a cook was to hell and gone, panic stricken as he looked. He was likely trying to figure out whether it was east or west he ought to strike out for before the news got to the crew.

Maria may have had a hitch in her git-along, but she hadn't lost any of her feistiness . . . or her female ways. The words were barely out of my mouth and the look had just come to Latch Key's face when she'd stepped right up alongside him. At first she threw me that hard case glance she was so good at when she got mad, but it was soon replaced by a sweet country woman smile. Negotiating is what she was about to do.

"Now, Black Jack, you ain't gonna tell 'em that, are you?"

"Got to, young lady. Day ain't come that they'd call Black Jack Hooker a liar."

"Why, you worthless old—" Any attempt at the fine art of bargaining was gone now. By God, she was going to hand me hell in a basket if that was what it took!

"Bad water is what I'm gonna say," I interrupted, showing a mite of temper my own self. "It was something in the water, and that's the truth." I leaned over and stuck out a bushy eyebrow, aimed it right at her. "Were I you, sis, I wouldn't try debating which shade tree I plant that truth under."

That shut her up right quick. It also brought a sigh of relief to Latch Key.

"Smart man would get his woman to going through his Arbuckles and checking for any more of those critters I jest seen and want to forget."

"You bet, boss," Latch Key said, giving Maria a nod as he said it. He was the cook on this drive, and he was back in charge.

Me, I took a hefty bite of that biscuit and went back to herding longhorns.

Chapter 17

Once you've had them on the trail for a good ten days or so, those ornery things with the long horns shouldn't stampede. That's what Tom Lang claimed. We'd been on the trail for more than half of the time it would take to get these cattle to market and so far we'd been lucky. Or maybe it was because there had been little if any rain thus far. Oh, the clouds had formed in the distance every once in a while, the wind accompanying them cooling off us all as it moved by, but it had never rained. The threat of it was all we'd been confronted with so far.

That afternoon the clouds formed again, a mass of dark gray that turned to pitch black by the time we circled the herd. A drop or two of rain had fallen in the afternoon and by the time we had the herd settled down, there seemed to be little doubt about what was in store for us that night. You can't always see it right off, but you can always tell when there's rain in the air. That smell is as distinctive as cookie's morning coffee or your mama's homemade soup. Once you smell it you know what it is, be it in sight or not.

"I hope cookie's got a hefty meal for us tonight, Black Jack," Lang said before we rode into camp. The clouds he was studying looked to be as dark as the frown on his forehead. "Gonna be a rough one tonight."

Then he shook his head in disgust. "Let's hope the water is better at this water hole."

He'd bought the story I fed him about bad water being the cause of the men's temporary illness that morning. The men had wolfed down the noon camp meal and begun to show more pep as the afternoon wore on. I had no doubt that Latch Key would be extra careful of the condition of his supplies from now on, for once was once but twice . . . well, that could get you to thinking.

I reckon it was Lang's comment that got me to wondering again. It all seemed innocent enough, the coffee and those vinegaroons, but something wasn't right about the whole thing. It was something I hadn't been able to put a finger on until just then. Arguing about that pot of coffee that morning, it hadn't appeared that Latch Key or his helper were any too sickly, not at all. Fact of the matter was that the both of them had gotten right feisty about my comments and were ready to go to war over them. On the other hand, Davy, Lang and his bunch, and my own boys and the rest were none too frisky. Shoot, those stragglers we were carrying at the drag had more energy than the crew itself did! I made a mental note to bring it up to Latch Key and his "wife" later on.

Tom Lang wasn't concerned so much about the quality of the food being served for supper as he was the quirks of nature and what they can do to a trail herd at night. I'd set around campfires with these Texas boys long enough to know that stampedes were the most dangerous risk on a trail drive. Putting up with the likes of some Indians wanting a cut of the herd was something they could allow. Even Indians on the warpath and the likes of Lem Cordova were tolerable to the extent of being part of what was expected along the trail. But a "stompede," as some of these lads were prone to call it for obvious reasons, well, that was the one nightmare a cowhand dreaded most. In many respects it was just as dangerous as standing up to the Lem Cordovas and Jared Watts of this world, the difference being that flannelmouths like Cordova and Watts could be dealt with more easily than ten thousand hoofs of spooked, panicky longhorns on the run. With flannelmouths you had an edge; tangling with scared cattle could be certain death.

Men like Tom Lang knew that a stampede was nothing but a losing situation for both the men and the herd. Hearing him talk around the fire these last couple of months, I'd discovered that during a stampede the herd would run at a wild pace for anywhere between a couple of miles and as many as fifteen before the animals wore themselves out. At that point, those four-legged animals you'd been so careful to feed and water would lose all of the fat they'd picked up during that run. That didn't improve the price you'd get for them at market any. But worse, you could lose some men and that meant everyone else would wind up pulling a bit more than they had before in the line of duty. Besides, after you work together for a while you get to feel like you're all one big family, no matter what your likes and dislikes are, and just like any family that loses a loved one, well, you'd miss the fellow who's gone. Believe me, I know. Back when I was a young buck a lot of us went to the mountains and spent the better part of a year together. On this trail drive I'd found out that it didn't matter whether it was two months or two years, these Texas boys and what Tom Lang had grudgingly referred to as us "misfits" at the start of the drive . . . we were working pretty well together. It wasn't love by any means, you understand, but I'd bet a dollar that if you asked any of the men in camp they'd admit to having a healthy respect for everyone else in the crew.

That being the case, Lang made sure Long John knew that each man was to have his mount saddled and ready to ride that night. Some might say he was being a mite cautious in doing that. Me, I knew better. The man wasn't doing anything more than making sure anyone critical of his orders lived long enough to gripe about them.

The food and coffee put everyone in a better mood that night, although I don't think there was a one of us who didn't have the sight of that big cloud formation stuck in the back of his mind. I did a little palavering after the meal, waiting for a good time to have a more serious talk with Latch Key and Maria. It was nightfall by the time I poured my last cup of coffee for the night and took a casual walk toward the chuck wagon. Latch Key and Maria were nowhere in sight, but they were nearby. At least that's who the voices I heard belonged to. Like I said, I never did like interrupting people who are talking away, so I came to a halt this side of the wagon, which put me well within earshot of them.

"I can't do it, Latch Key, I just can't." The way those words came out they were mixed with fear and a bit of remorse. "The man saved my hide. I don't care what kind of blackmail Jared Watts is holding on me, I just can't do it."

Silence, then a sigh from the cook.

"Know what you mean. Man saved my reputation today, he did. You'd have to go a mighty far piece for that kind of treatment. I'd have to agree with you, ma'am, but a thousand dollars is a lot of money to kill for. He's already given me half of it. Long as Hooker don't show up at the end of the trail, I'll get the other five hundred."

Hearing that nearly had me gagging on the coffee I was sipping! The fact that Jared Watts had used some personal blackmail to get Maria to go along on the drive I already knew. She had told me that on our ride into Two Dog with Lem Cordova and his boys. She was to go along on the drive, masquerading as Latch Key's wife, and do as much as she could to disrupt it. Part of that disruption was to have come from that one item on her shopping list that I convinced her to forget about. A tincture of poison is what it was. Jared Watts was the man who had found her when she was starving, used her, abused her, and tried to turn her into a lady of the evening, if you get my drift. He had gotten her to agree to ride along with us by threatening to tell her father and brothers all about her sordid past if she didn't. Bad as the menfolk in her family were, he'd be signing her death warrant for sure.

What Jared Watts didn't know was that he was the one in for the surprise, for during that conversation we had on the way to Two Dog, you might say I changed Maria's mind some. Told her to up and leave Watts once this drive was over with, I did; that me and the boys would keep him from doing her any harm and her father and brothers as well, if need be.

What shocked me now was hearing from Latch Key's own mouth was that Jared Watts had hired him to kill me! The only reason I could think of for that was pure revenge. Watts should know that even if I were killed Tom Lang would take the herd through to trail's end. At first I didn't know what to think, for I'd hired the cook my own self. Was this whole thing a set up, me hiring him as the cook for this drive? Had my murder been planned before or after I'd hired him? Or was Latch Key simply being windy to impress the woman? It wouldn't be the first time such a stunt had been pulled. While all of that was rushing through my mind, the two had fallen silent, but only for a moment.

"Latch Key, why don't you call me Maria?" she asked. I had a notion she was smiling the way she did just before she'd kissed me that one time. "We're supposed to be man and wife, you know."

"Well, I . . . you'd only think—" More silence, only this time I *knew* they were kissing one another.

While I was debating whether I ought to barge in and give them both a good thrashing, drops of rain began to fall. The afternoon had brought only a sprinkle, but when a drop caused quite a splash in my coffee cup, now, well, I knew they were getting bigger; knew it wouldn't be long before we'd have us a real thunder boomer on our hands.

The only other movement in the camp was that of the crew putting on their slickers. It was then I heard the damndest clap of thunder that ever existed. Bold as could be, and it was followed by a second one, this one carrying a huge streak of lightning with it. A crashing sound shook the air and I thought I saw that lightning bolt strike the far side of the herd.

"Boys, the herd's a-running!" I heard Davy yell from the near side of those steers.

"All hands and the cook!!" Tom Lang's booming voice sounded. Normally the cook had little to do with the cattle on a trail drive, but when you heard what Lang had just yelled, why, son, you could bet you had a real emergency that called for every able-bodied man in the outfit to pitch in.

My talk with Latch Key and Maria would have to wait.

Having those horses near at hand saved the day. Why, I do believe that the only time I've ever seen men move faster was when they were being shot at, and this was proving to be just as deadly a game. I must have been the only one who didn't have a slicker, but hell I never had carried one to begin with. Been through more rainy seasons, washouts, and floods than any ten men will likely see in a lifetime, I have. So getting to my horse was all I needed to do right now.

Contrary to what you might think, no herd of cattle ever runs together in a night stampede. They'll scatter and go around big objects in their way before coming back together and trying to find the direction of the wind to run against. Lang and his crew must have been out toward the front, trying to get a fix on that leader and turn him into a circling motion so all these critters would do was gather together like one big ball of grandma's yarn. Luckily, we'd been heading into a north wind all day and it hadn't changed yet, so maybe that would help slow the stampede. What caught my eye was how a good part of the herd was still to the rear of the chuck wagon, even if it was off to one side. All we'd need would be to have these red-eyed critters take a notion to head in this direction and wipe out the chuck wagon in the process.

Latch Key noticed it, too. Quicker than lightning through a gooseberry bush, he was pushing Maria atop the seat of the wagon. If he was thinking the same as me, he'd want the woman to control the chuck wagon, which, like the cowhands' horses, was also hitched and ready to go tonight. And control was exactly what would

be needed, for that team was just as skittish as those
longhorns. Maria had a handful to take care of as soon
as her git up end hit the seat and she grabbed the reins.
The grizzled cook was about to head for the supply
wagon when Matthew appeared out of nowhere.

"No!" he yelled, waving a hand at Latch Key and
jumping from his own horse to the supply wagon. "Hold
'em steady on the chuck and I'll put this 'un around."
Waiting never was one of Matthew's strong suits and
before you knew it his big frame was centered on the
driver's box, moving that supply wagon around so it
crossed the front of the chuck wagon like the top line of
a T. Fixing to make up one of those big objects that the
herd would wind up going around instead of through,
that's what he was doing.

"Hang on to this," I heard Diah command, then saw
him hand Maria the reins of Matthew's horse as the
cook took charge of his chuck wagon.

God only knew whether this mad idea would work,
but you don't get nothing done unless you give it a try.
Besides, if we were fated to get mutilated by this herd, it
might as well be there as anywhere.

Matthew had his hands full managing that team, which
left only me and Diah with nothing to do. That's how it
looked anyway. I reckon you could say us Hookers tend
to rise to the occasion when it calls for it, and that
means thinking the same, too. I swear that Diah and I
gave each other a glance at the exact same moment. A
group of cattle had separated from the main herd and
were headed our way at a dead run.

"Time to see what kind of stopping power this brass
boy of yours has, Pa," my boy yelled out.

I never did comment for it was then that we shoul-
dered those Winchesters and each shot a couple or three
charging steers in the center of the forehead. The first
two were dead as soon as the bullets hit them, but the
force they had already built up carried them to about
fifteen yards in front of the supply wagon. The second
pair fell behind them and the stampeding herd parted
like the Red Sea after Moses gave the order. Diah smiled

and I gave him a wink like I had in the old days when he was a youngster and had done a good job.

"Looks like we saved our bacon in more ways than one," Matthew said, seeing that the chuck wagon was still in one piece when the herd was gone.

"That sounds like what them back east folk would call an observation, son." If I was making light of it, you can bet it was because I felt a pure sigh of relief go through me at having come through this whole thing alive.

When Latch Key and Maria assured us they could handle everything, the boys and I lit out looking for the herd and the rest of the crew. It was maybe five or six miles ahead that Lang and his men were circling the still nervous longhorns. The Texans had all made it through the ordeal, if my head count was correct, but I could only spot Bud giving them a hand.

"Where's everyone else?" I asked Lang.

"Long John's out there somewhere," he said, pointing out into the night. "Looking for the damned remuda. Ain't seen the chief or the other Juarez."

"Likely out looking for strays, I reckon."

"Not hardly, Pa," Matthew said, his eyes gazing at Eagle Feather slowly riding toward us in the darkness. Beside him walked a horse, its rider slumped over in the saddle. He didn't have his sombrero on, but I was giving odds the man on that horse was Jorge Juarez.

I was right.

"Back shot," was all the chief said, coming to a halt.

Lang was the first to inspect the body.

"Well, I'll be damned." It was the closest I'd heard the tough-talking Texan come to being astonished at anything. No one said it, but if I'd had any takers I'd have been picking up my winnings, for it was indeed Bud's brother.

"Most of us are," Diah said. I don't know how he could make it out in that little amount of light, but my younger boy had seen something in my own face and was getting snoopy about it. "You are right, Pa? You're looking kinda—"

"Fine, boy, just fine," I growled in anger. Without another word I wheeled my horse around and found something else to do.

Hell, I wasn't going to tell them that it was Jorge Juarez I'd traded my nighthawk position with so I could do some talking to our cook and his helper, a talk that never did take place.

Chapter 18

We spent all night rounding up what strays were near-by. Most of us anyway. Bud Juarez caught up with me soon after he found out what had happened to his brother. Madder than hell wouldn't come anywhere close to describing the look on his face. Out for blood is what he was. I reckon he knew as well as I did that no streak of lightning ever left a hole like the one in his brother's back. A long gun put it there; Jorge would never have let anyone get that close to him with a six-shooter. Besides, I was thinking back on what I thought I'd seen on the far side of the herd when that lightning struck and started the stampede. That second bolt had landed far from the herd, now that I thought about it. Yet the cracking sound had come from the same area as the first lightning strike and it was that flash, that sound that had registered in my mind. Plays funny tricks on you, your upstairs does. Sees and hears things that only seem important later on. For example, I only knew now what that flash I'd seen had been.

"He was murdered, Hooker! My brother was murdered!" Hard, mean, and just a mite of over the edge, that was how he sounded. Can't say as I blamed him one bit either. But I was carrying around some guilt of my own that concerned his brother's death.

"I know, Bud, I know." The rain that had fallen

during the stampede stopped just as quickly as it had started, almost as if the Maker had planned the whole event. Well, maybe that rainstorm was of His making, but I had a storm of my own a-brewing and it didn't have anything to do with rain. "Find yourself a place you want to bury Jorge and we'll get it done. I'll be at the chuck wagon seeing can I dig up a shovel or two."

I reckon we both understood what had to be done and went our separate ways without another word. Bud, he knew I wasn't about to let what happened to his brother go unaccounted for. I was hoping he'd work with me on it instead of taking off on some wild revenge hunt that might cost him his life.

"Wasn't as bad as I thought it would be," Latch Key was saying when I rode into the camp. He and Maria looked to be in high spirits, dragging out some of the deadwood he carried for such occasions from under the chuck wagon. I dismounted, not saying a word.

When I was close enough to him, I hit him. Hard. Only once, mind you, but hard enough to send him reeling back into the side of the chuck wagon. Maria dropped the piece of deadwood she was carrying and stepped back toward the end of the wagon.

"What in the hell—" the cook began.

"A good man's dead because of you." A growl in my voice? Not hardly, son. That was pure hatred, the killing kind.

"Killed?" Latch Key was confused. I'd caught him off guard when I hit him and he was just as puzzled now. "We lose one of the crew? What the hell are you talking about?"

"Didn't lose no one once that stampede started, Latch Key, but we lost a man just *before* it got started, ary I miss my guess."

"Who?" Maria asked in a concerned voice.

"Jorge. He took my shift on the nighthawk so's I could stay in camp a mite longer and talk to you two lovebirds. Right interesting conversation you two were holding afore the storm hit."

"You mean you were eaves—" Latch Key was about

to come at me from his position in front of the chuck wagon, but bringing my Brass Boy up and jabbing him in the gut with it made him think again.

"No, mister. You two were talking and I was listening and that's the all of it. What you and me got to palaver about now is the subject of your conversation, namely *me*." I pushed the Winchester a little harder into his stomach, saw a paleness come to his face as he realized what I knew.

My anger at Latch Key was what I had on my mind now, which is a good example of what I'd been hoping Bud Juarez wouldn't do. Hell, I'd become so caught up in what the cook had been saying about me earlier that I'd blocked out everything and everyone around me. And that was about to prove fatal.

"Drop your rifle, Black Jack." I was suddenly aware of Maria's presence, particularly since she had a Colt in her hand at full cock and it was pointed at me. I would've told her I was willing to gamble on the hand I was holding, but an ace kicker stepped in and did it for me.

"You are *una bonita senorita*, Maria," Bud said, stepping into the light across the camp from the woman. "*Si*, a very pretty lady. But if you do not put the *pistola* away, you will be dead." I caught a glimpse of him out of the corner of my eye. He had no gun in hand, didn't have the drop on her as I'd suspected from the way he spoke. His hands were simply at his sides. Calm as could be is how he appeared.

"I could kill you where you stand, mister. Tell him how good a shot I am, Black Jack." Maria was the one who was getting fidgety now, more than a hint of uncertainty in her voice.

"That she is, Bud. Wouldn't argy it a-tall," I said.

"Do you think I care, senorita? *Mi hermano*, my brother, is dead. Do you think it matters now if I die, too? Shoot if you must, but know that when you do you will be dead also."

I didn't think Bud was bluffing, not at all. The worried look on Maria's face was telling me that she'd gotten the same impression. Still it was her choice to make. She could die making a fight of it or back down and lose a bit of pride. The way her upper lip started to quiver, I had a feeling that it wouldn't be long before that nervousness moved on down to the pistol she held in her hand. I've got to tell you, hoss, I never did care to die an accidental death.

"She's a good shot, Bud," I said as I lowered the rifle. "But she ain't a killer. Not like some I know." I was dearly hoping she would figure I was talking about Jared Watts and not Latch Key when I said that.

There was a long silence before she uncocked the six-gun and slowly lowered it to her side. "No," she said, although I could barely make it out.

"Cookie, you get some Arbuckles on the fire and be quick about it," I said as calmly as I could. "We got us some palavering to do before the crew comes in."

And that we did. One of the rules around camp was that there would be no drinking, but after what the four of us had been through that night, well, we made an exception to the rule and each took a long pull on that bottle of sour mash Maria kept hidden somewhere. Warmed us up until the coffee was ready. It wasn't long after we'd filled our cups with fresh, hot coffee that Lang and most of the crew returned. By then I'd found out what I needed to know.

The cook of a trail outfit hadn't necessarily spent his lifetime making six-shooter coffee, biscuits, and deep-dish apple pie. No, sir. More than likely he had a past that included a whole variety of work he'd done before putting on an apron. He might now be too busted up to break any more broncs; or a used-to-was mountain man like some I knew; or had run afoul of the law in some other territory. The latter was the case with Latch Key. Oh, he'd worked as a cook for a few outfits all right, but it was when he killed a man that he'd moved on. If he were to be believed—and I wasn't entirely sure I did believe him—this job with me was the one he was hoping would put him on what mama called the "straight and narrow." His instincts had brought out that gun in the saloon that first day I'd met him and for that I was grateful. Trouble was that one of those yahoos in the saloon, one of Jared Watts' men, had recognized him and passed it on to the boss man. That led to Watts himself meeting secretly with Latch Key that same day, making him the thousand-dollar offer for my hide and arranging to have Maria accompany him as his wife to carry out her own little mission.

"There, it's all out." The cook said it with some relief when he'd finished his story. "You do what you want, Hooker. Tell me to leave the territory and I will. Right now. Pick up what little's mine and go, I will. Turn me over to Juarez iffen you think it'll bring back his brother. But I honest to God didn't kill him and I'd already changed my mind about trying to take you out as well." The last sentence seemed to take the steam out of him as he found the ground better to look at than me. "I'm just tired, Hooker. Tired of being pulled one way and the other, tired of being on the run."

You know something, hoss? I do believe he meant it.

"How you gonna explain keeping that five hundred dollars to Jared Watts? He strikes me as the kind of rattlesnake that would try to hunt you down harder than anyone else you'll ever run into." I knew that to be the truth because of what had happened to me since I'd won the ranchers' business rather than him.

"Hell, I'll give it back to him when we get back to Texas."

It was then Tom Lang rode into the new site with his men. "Your boys said they'd keep an eye on the herd, Black Jack." To Bud, he said, "Sorry 'bout your brother, Juarez. Don't you fret none, though. Once we get through taking this herd to the end of the trail, we'll track down the bastard that done it, me and the boys." Seeing the downtrodden look on Latch Key's face, he added, "Coffee that bad?"

"No," the cook replied. "Hooker here's trying to figure out whether to shoot me or hang me." He said it looking straight at me.

It was obvious that neither Lang nor his men had a

notion of what we were talking about and for right now I intended to keep it that way.

"Hell, I wouldn't do that," I said, tossing a shovel to Bud and mounting up. "Need me a cook too bad for that. But was I you, boys, I'd keep me an eye out for vinegaroons."

Lang and his men were still confused, but like I said, it wasn't the right time for them to know all that I did. You might say that I'd also answered Latch Key's demand for a decision, in my own little way, of course.

For right now he could stay.

Bud and I, we buried his brother that night.

Chapter 19

A couple of weeks later we reached what the crew had been looking forward to for some time, trail's end. And I'll tell you, hoss, those last two weeks sure did seem like the easiest ones of the drive because there was no more trouble, from Mother Nature or humans. Not that I wasn't expecting it.

About a week before we reached Sedalia, Missouri, we picked up an outrider. The chief was the first to spot him, then me. It wasn't one of those Osage who were prone to making trouble in the Indian Territory we'd recently left. No, it was a white man all right. The only thing that kept me from going after him was a desire to avoid as much trouble as I could. Lordy, but we'd had more than our share of it on this drive, and I wouldn't go blaming the presence of a woman for all of it either. So if he wanted to mind his own business, well, that was fine with me. By the time we settled that herd in on a grassy area south of the cowtown, he had disappeared. That, too, was fine with me.

Tom Lang, my boys, and I took a ride into Sedalia to seek out the buyers we'd been told would be looking for us. Turned out there were plenty of them looking for beef to buy and paying top dollar for it. That was one reason Lang and I had stopped south of the city. By our tally we'd lost upward of a hundred head along the way and the stampede had taken some of the meat off of the longhorns we had left. The grazing had gotten better the closer we got to our destination, and the herd had slowly picked up some of the weight it had lost. One last good graze and watering wouldn't hurt the selling price of these ornery beasts we'd been on the trail with the past three months. It would mean more money for all of us, so no one complained about waiting a day or two more before celebrating in the city.

There were precious few other locations for a man to take his cattle in this state. From Sedalia the cattle would be shipped by the Missouri Pacific Railroad either west to Kansas City or east to St. Louis for slaughter. The way the railroads had been making their way west since the middle of the war, there seemed little doubt that other locations would soon be opening up. One such I'd heard mention of was a place called Ellsworth over in Kansas, although I'd never been there. For the moment, Sedalia would be fine, thank you.

Riding into town I saw a man sitting in a chair outside the office of the local law, dressed in what I'd heard called the garb of a river rat gambler. Black hat, coat, and trousers covering a clean white shirt and vest. Tipping his hat to the ladies who passed him by, he was. I had him figured for one of the tinhorn gamblers that frequented towns like this. Yes, sir. Only thing that made me take him in twice was that face of his. I could have sworn I'd seen it before. No, it couldn't have been that Hickok lad I'd had a run in with. Could it? I dismissed the thought as we found a saloon to tie our mounts in front of.

"After this long we need at least one drink," I said. "Hell, I'll even buy 'em."

"As much grief as you've given me, Black Jack, you'd *better* buy 'em," Lang said. A hint of a smile had come to his face and I had a hunch he was as glad to see this town as I was.

Unless you were in St. Louis, old Taos, or that Spanish City of the Angels out in California, why, any city or town west of the Mississippi was young by comparison.

Sedalia was no different than some of those places we'd been in Texas and the Nations; it had been around a year or two but it was still mighty rough at the edges.

We bellied up to the bar of that saloon in short order. More than likely it was not having a beer in so long that made that first one taste so good. We hadn't even finished the first glass when we were approached by some men looking for herds to buy up. They bought the second round and offered twice as much as either Lang or I had figured we could ever get for one of those mangy longhorns. Struck a deal right then and there, we did. The buyers would be out the following day to look over the herd and talk a cash-on-the-barrelhead price. When they left, we were feeling real confident we'd made a sale.

Feeling good about something had never lasted too awful long on this trail drive. Today was no exception.

"Bringing a herd in, are you, boys?" It was the fancified gambler I'd spied across the street. He was pleasant enough in his manner, but then, most of those fellows are; for starters, anyway.

"Yeah, what's it to you?" Lang was taking the man in, noticing that he was near his size and maybe a mite heftier. In other words, Lang was going back to being himself.

"You'll have to overlook our friend." I smiled a bit apologetically. "Took him three months to get used to us humans. When we git back to Texas, I'm gonna turn him out into the wilderness again." Lang didn't find a lot of humor in that, but like I say, I wasn't looking for any fights. Hell, heading him off at the pass was the only way to keep him out of a fight now. "Say," I continued, "do I know you from somewhere? Look mighty familiar, you do, son."

He shrugged noncommittally, that easy smile coming to his face again. "No," he said, the smile broadening as he looked me over from top to bottom, "but I think I know you. I'd bet a dollar you're Hooker. Black Jack, isn't it?"

I cocked a suspicious eye at him, never being one who

cared to be left in the dark. Tends to obfusticate me.
Digging into my memory, trying to place him, well, I
reckon I didn't pay much attention to the batwings being
pushed open as hard as they were.

I didn't have to see him to recognize him. The gruff,
bitter voice of Jared Watts was picking up volume as he
headed my way. He pushed the young man before me
aside, planting his feet dead in front of me, hands on
hips, defiant as hell. The gambler, if that's what he was,
didn't seem too shaken, not even appearing to lose his
balance. Must've gotten used to being pushed around
like that. A lot of the tinhorns I'd run across while
playing poker were long on talk and short on laying
down their hole card when it came to backing a hand or
being a man.

"That cook of yours, Latch Key, says you've been
saying some mighty bad things 'bout me, Hooker." Hard
and mean as ever, Watts was looking for a fight, pushing
for one real hard. Fact is, I'd been expecting to find him
here in Sedalia. Hell, you would, too, if you'd had all of
the problems we did on that drive.

"Well, I'll tell you, Watts, I don't know what it is
Latch Key's been saying, but ary it's the truth I'd figure
you wouldn't like it much." I added a taunting smile to
the words, saw the man go blood red in the face. He
wasn't the only one in the room who knew how to push.

"Gents, if you've got a fight, you're going to have to
take it outside, and I mean outside the *city limits*." The
smile was gone from the young man's face, replaced now by
a look of authority. Jared Watts, he didn't care one
whit.

"Do you know who I am, mister?" he sounded off.
Real self-centered, Watts was.

"Well now, friend, that was going to be my very next
question," the other man said. Clean shaven as he was,
the furrows on his forehead said a lot about where he'd
been. Believe me, I know a war map when I see one.
Pushing thirty, I'd say, somewhere in between the ages
of my own boys. Whatever the age, he didn't look so
easygoing anymore.

"Watts, Jared Watts. Now, stay outta this, boy, it ain't none of your concern." He'd barely looked at the younger man, he was that intent on cussing and threatening me. But the gambler seemed just as intent on getting involved. I've got to tell you, hoss, that what he was doing wasn't the healthiest thing for a man to do in these parts. A man's fights were his own private affair, and stepping into one was liable to get a body in a lot more trouble than he'd originally intended.

"My name's Callahan. Jim Callahan." If it was supposed to mean something to Watts, it didn't. But the name jogged my memory, putting a few things in place. I knew now where it was I'd seen the lad, except it wasn't him I'd seen.

"Well, bully for you," Watts said, taking a step back and turning to face Callahan, a perturbed look about him. It was evident he had come for one thing and was being delayed by another and clearly didn't like it. No, sir. "And just what in hell makes you want to get tangled up in this?"

"This," Callahan said, pulling back the left side of his black frock coat, revealing the badge of a marshal pinned to his vest and a holstered Colt's Army Model .44. "And this," he added, just as slowly pulling back the right side of the coat, letting all who cared to take a gander see the matching pistol on the right hip. "They pay me for keeping the peace around here, friend, and right now you don't look too awful peaceful. Why don't you take a nice long walk, and don't stop 'til you get past the city limits." A flash of anger shone in Jared Watts' eyes, but young Callahan was as cool as could be about it. "It would be a mistake to do otherwise, Mister Watts. Maybe even your last one."

"We'll see about that," the craggy Texan said before doing a quick about-face and leaving the saloon.

"He'll be back," Matthew said.

"Not if he knows what's good for him," Jim Callahan said.

"Sean Callahan, wasn't it!" I said when the tension had broken and things got back to normal in the barroom.

"That's a fact, Mister Hooker." The marshal smiled over a beer. "According to Sean, you and he did some campaigning with Carson down around Adobe Walls. Got a lot of sand, he says. And looks that'd be hard to miss." He shook his head at this last comment, looking me over from the neck up, or what he could see past my whiskers.

He was right about me and Sean Callahan, who, unless memory fails me, was a cousin or some kind of relative to the man next to me now. Sean would be about Diah's age and just as frisky. This other Callahan, well, he ran long on guts, too, if what I'd seen was any indication.

"You fellas ain't looking to make trouble here, are you?" he asked in a neighborly way.

"Just selling a herd of longhorns," Diah commented.

"That's right," Lang said, sipping his beer.

"There is one other thing, marshal," I said, taking another swig of what was passable brew. "If we can find us a private table, I've got a story to tell you. Might not concern you 'cepting for two things."

"Oh?" I had his curiosity aroused.

"Yeah. It has to do with a man of mine getting murdered."

"And?"

"And I think Jared Watts had it done. Can't prove it yet, but . . ."

Callahan ordered two more beers.

"Let's find that table, Mister Hooker."

Chapter 20

I told Callahan the whole story, everything from offering my services on the trail drive to my latest run-in with Jared Watts, a rattlesnake of a man who I believed was involved in damn near every mishap we'd come upon in the last three months. I reckon that Callahan boy, Sean, the one I'd fought beside with Carson and his New Mexico Volunteers, had turned out to have a grudging respect for me. I say that because Jim Callahan took a lot of what I said at face value, which was a mite unusual for a lawman.

"Can't *prove* he's behind all of this, you understand, Jim," I said in exasperation, "but I know this type and, by God, it's Jared Watts all right. Ary I had the cattle money in hand I'd bet the whole wad on it."

"From what you say, I wouldn't doubt it, but"—here the lawman gave a hopeless shrug—"like you say, there ain't nothing you can pin to him." He sipped his beer in silence. Me, I wasn't about to interrupt him; why, that's when you get some of your best thinking done, son, mulling over a beer. "Tell you what, Black Jack, you let me do some checking on this fancy new telegraph they're all bragging about. A couple of those fellas' names sound familiar that you came across on the trail. You say those buyers are going to take a look see at your herd tomorrow morning. That means that if they've got the cash to pay you, it's likely in one of our banks. You check with me tomorrow afternoon when you come to town to pick up your pay and I'll let you know what I find out."

"Thanks, Jim, I appreciate it," I said, offering the man my hand as I rose to leave.

"That being the case, Black Jack, why don't you do me a favor?"

"Name it." I was taking a liking to this young man.

"Keep that fight you've got with Watts out of town. I know it don't look like much, but we've got women and youngsters in Sedalia now and I'd like to keep 'em alive. Like I said, it's what they pay me for."

"You bet." Nothing unreasonable about that request.

The talk around the fire that night was of the sale of the herd and the celebration that would take place afterwards, when everyone got paid. I did some storytelling about that fight we'd had at Adobe Walls back in '64, mentioning how the marshal of Sedalia was related to a youngster I'd fought beside.

"Oh, yeah, Sean Callahan," Long John said with a smile. You'd have thought he'd been there at the battle his own self, the way he said it. "I know him, too."

Now, that threw me. "Run that by me one more time, son."

But he did know Sean Callahan, and Carson as well. Said he'd met and talked with both of them, but for the life of me I couldn't figure out when and why, and asked.

"Some of us were lucky before the war," Long John said with a bit of remorse. "A few of us escaped slavery through the Underground Railroad. I was one of them. I was fortunate enough to get a decent education, reading, writing, and all.

"There was a man who died at Adobe Walls, Black Jack. Bigger than me, taller than me. Hannibal was his name. I never did find out until after the war was over. I'd been travelling around, trying to find him. It wasn't long ago that I met up with Sean Callahan and found out what happened to Hannibal. Talking with Carson I met up with Eagle Feather and we took to tracking you down.'' That wasn't what I had expected to hear and I cocked that leery eye at him.

"They speak highly of you, Sean and Carson," Long John went on. "They say you were there when Hannibal died, when he was killed. I was just going to stop by and say thanks for being there with him, but I reckon I got involved with the whole lot of you." He smiled warmly, taking in each and every man at the fire. "I'm glad I came along."

"This Hannibal a friend of yours?" I asked.

"No, Black Jack, it was a bit more than that." He got up, gave the one remaining Juarez a sad look and said, "Believe me, Bud, I know how you feel," before walking away from the fire.

Hannibal had been his brother.

Family runs pretty strong with folks out here. I know it does with us Hookers. I had a feeling the same was true of the Callahans I'd met so far. Bud did his work just as well, but with half the enthusiasm he'd put into it before Jorge was killed. Long John had shown how much family meant to him when he bared his soul to us that night around the campfire. As for the chief, well, if you'd been out here any length of time you'd know better than to even question family relationships in the life of an Indian. Some of them were strange, true, but they were tight bonds that were seldom if ever broken.

Being on that trail the three months that we had, we'd grown to be an informal family of our own. Riding for the brand is what some would call it. Oddly enough there was one more family tie that none of us outsiders—those other than the Texans—knew about. We found out about it the following day after the buyers had looked over our herd, made a better than expected offer, and left to get their money together in town, which I planned to ride in and collect a bit later. It was also then that hell started taking a holiday.

He rode into camp free and easy. When the chief nodded, I knew he was the outrider we'd seen. His arm was in a sling and he didn't look all that well. But he had

gall, I'll give him that. It was Carl, the youngster in
Cordova's crowd I'd tangled with; it was he who had
ridden down that back alley with a bullet high in his
back and another in his arm. He might have gotten the
bullets out, but he sure didn't look like he was healing
all that well.

"Looking kinda peaked, mister," Davy said, helping
the man dismount.

"Could use some coffee if you've got it," Carl replied
with a sheepish grin. Davy got him a cup and poured
coffee as Carl plunked his get up end on the ground near
the fire. Mostly a man would squat by a fire, but this
hombre was too worn out to do so from the looks of
him.

"You picked a sure way of dying, riding in here like
this," Lang said upon seeing him. I had a hunch Lang's
memory was damn near as good as mine.

"Ain't so sure I ain't halfway there right now." The
wounded man grinned. He sipped the coffee, waited a
second, gulped some more. "Thought I'd try to make up
for what I done before I go."

It was hard to believe, coming from a man who'd been
a party to killing a lawman the way Gar Tucker had been
murdered.

"That so," I said, leaning against the chuck wagon,
enjoying my own cup of coffee.

"You can believe it or not," he said, suddenly gagging, spitting up some of the liquid he'd just swallowed,
a gob of blood accompanying it. "I just came to have
my say."

"Then have at it, son," I said.

"After you left Two Dog I snuck back in one night.
Found the doctor and made him patch me up." He
coughed again, spitting up more blood. A small amount,
mind you, but it was blood just the same. "Either he
ain't much on patch-up work or my wound is a mite past
repair." Any man in camp who was listening to him
knew it was the latter for the doctor there in Two Dog
had done a fine job of fixing up Maria's foot. In fact, she

was getting around halfway decent now, even if she still had a hitch in her git along.

"I've got better things to do than listen to this," Tom Lang said bitterly. It was obvious he had no love for such a man as Carl.

"You might want to hear it," Carl said, this time aiming his words right at the tall Texan. "Fella named Watts has been following your herd all the way from Texas." This wasn't anything Tom Lang or the rest of us didn't know by now, so all the man got was an impatient look. "Lem Cordova came back and sprung Sandy from that Two Dog jail, according to the sawbones." Sandy would have been the fair-haired lad Jorge'd rigged the shotgun up in front of in his jail cell when that fandango was over. "Cordova joined up with Watts not long afterward. I reckon both of 'em got the same thing in mind." The cough was deeper this time and it was me he was looking at when he added, "Killin' you."

That might not be the solid evidence Jim Callahan or any other lawman would need to jail a man, but it made everything clear to me! That beaver hat of mine had a wide, flat brim to it, not unlike a Mexican sombrero. Being just past sundown, whoever it was that had killed Jorge—and I was now certain it was Cordova—had nothing more than an outline to go by to recognize his target. It was pure luck that the storm had built up as badly as it had that day, camouflaging for a while what was really taking place, *someone trying to kill me*. The stampede had enabled the killer to get away without being noticed, something else that had worked in his favor.

"Son, how would you feel about telling your story to the town marshal here?" Hell, it may not have been much, but it would be something to get Jim Callahan started.

"Sure," Carl said without hesitation. "Who knows, maybe I'll even find a decent sawbones." He was starting to smile when a shot rang out and he slumped forward, back shot as dead as Jorge had been. It wasn't a split second before the second shot cracked and Davy, who had been squatted down next to Carl, was falling to the ground, too.

For a second there we were all hugging the earth, not sure if there was more death on the way or not. Tom Lang was the one who first decided he didn't give a damn and rushed to Davy's side. The boy wasn't dead, but he wasn't far from it either, the bullet having landed head on in the side of his back. Lang had the lad in his arms quick as you please, but all he saw was a confused look on Davy's face.

"Why'd they shoot me, Tom? I didn't—"

"I don't know, kid," Lang said in a soft, sad voice. I was half expecting him to cry. "I don't know." But he was talking to a dead man, and knew it most of all. He was laying the boy gently down on the ground when Matthew came a-running.

"Two of 'em hightailing it, Pa. One had a bowler hat."

"It's Cordova," I said, needing no more identification.

"When I get through with the sonofabitch, you'll be saying he *was* Cordova." An ugly growl was what came out of Tom Lang's mouth as he took a half dozen huge strides, forked his mount, and headed in the same direction the killers had gone. Toward town.

"You been wanting to fight for so long," I said to my own young 'uns, "well, grab up them Winchesters, git your mounts, and we'll see just how brassy you boys feel now." It was one of those challenges you pass on to a son when he's spent more time than he needed talking about his bigness. They took it just the way I meant it and were soon on their horses.

"Slim, you and the rest of these Texicans get out there and watch that herd," I ordered. "Them shots are going to have made 'em mighty skittish by now."

"Got it, boss." The toothpick nodded. "Anything else?"

"Yeah. Why's Lang taking the boy's death so hard? Coulda cared less when Jorge Juarez got killed."

"Jorge Juarez wasn't his brother," Slim said before putting himself in motion.

That explained a lot, although I'd never heard Lang or any of the others mention the relationship between Davy and the trail boss. Davy must've wanted to be treated like an equal and without favor; if that was his wish, he'd gotten it, for Lang had been hard but fair to every one of us. Can't fault a man for that.

I also knew that if Lang got drawn into a shooting match in Sedalia, it wouldn't make a tinker's damn to Callahan how the fight got started. I got the impression that the law was the law with that man and you listened to him or went to jail. Mad as Tom Lang was, I'd lay money he'd go up against the marshal even if he did succeed in killing Lem Cordova.

Me, my boys, Bud, and Long John were the ones who left the camp, seeing if we could save Lang's hide. We were halfway to town when I heard a couple of horses to my rear, and pulled to a halt to see Latch Key and Maria trying to catch up with us.

"What the hell do you two want?" I demanded.

"Got some coin here belongs to Watts," Latch Key said. "I recall rightly, I told you I'd be giving it back to him."

"You're going to need all the help you can get, Black Jack," the woman said. "I know Watts' ways and one way or another he's gonna set you up for a killing." Gutsy talk for a woman with a hobbled leg.

"Now, you listen to me, sis," I said, jabbing a finger through the air at her, "this ain't no Sunday go-to-meeting social we're walking into! More like a corpse and cartridge party is what it is. You figure you're that tough, turn that steed 'round and get back to camp. Someone steals my coffee pot I'm going to hold you responsible!"

The woman was daft! First she cocked her eye at me as though she were trying to imitate me; damn but that looked silly. Then she stuck her tongue out at me like some schoolgirl would to a teacher. Then she turned tail and lit a shuck.

Getting rid of Maria was the least of my problems. It struck me as we continued toward town that what she'd

said was likely right. If Callahan didn't know every man
in Jared Watts' bunch of coyotes, why, they could ride
into town one or two at a time and spread themselves
out until Watts made his appearance. It seemed like his
kind of style. I said as much to those with me, instruct-
ing Matthew to start checking the saloons on one side of
the street, Diah on the other when we reached the edge
of town. I figured Lang for the kind of bloodhound who
would go from one saloon to another until he found his
man and then give him hell.

Bud and Long John were there one minute and gone
the next as we entered town, which left me and Latch
Key to pull up in front of the marshal's office.

"Your Jared Watts is an interesting man, Black Jack,"
Callahan said when I barged in. "Bad as some of the
carpetbaggers out here. Makes a habit of buying the law
here and there down his way." I remembered the lawman who had been part of the lynch mob who'd been
after Latch Key and knew that what the marshal said
was likely true.

"Do tell."

"I found one lawman down there that I *know* can't be
bought," he continued. "How would you feel about
taking Watts back with you, Black Jack? You can get
your crew to testify about all the chaos he's caused. It'll
help convict him if the charges I have ain't strong
enough."

"Well . . ." I drew it out, not sure I liked the idea at
all.

"Tell you what, Black Jack, you look like an honest
man. Consider yourself deputized. Watts oughtta be somewhere out on the edge of town."

"Won't have to go that far," Latch Key said from just
outside the door. A gander out into the street proved he
was right for there was Jared Watts with a handful of his
gunmen, reining in at the saloon across the way.

"You didn't tell me this was a feud and not just a
fight, Hooker," the lanky marshal said, pulling on his
jacket and positioning his hat just so. Cocky, his manner
was.

"You didn't give a chance to say so," was the only reason I could give. But he was right. A feud is what it was about to turn into. The rest of Watts' gunmen had started to gather behind him on the opposite side of the street.

"Watts, I need to talk to you," the marshal called. By God, the man didn't waste any time. Stepped right out into the street, he did. But he wasn't alone, not by a long sight.

Bud stepped out of the side alley to his right, those two big Remingtons holstered but ready for use. At the other end of the block and farther away, the big black figure of Long John stepped out, leaning against the side of a building, rifle at port arms. And, of course, Latch Key and I were behind Callahan. From what I could see, the odds were pretty close to two-to-one against us.

"You're going back to Texas, Watts, but you ain't packing no flame throwers or bringing along any hired protection." Like I said, Callahan had guts. You knew that just by seeing the way Watts and the gunmen with him gazed at the marshal. To them he was totally mad. "Now all of you take off the hardware or I'm going to put enough lead in the lot of you to make taking it out again a paying proposition." They were big words this man was talking.

People started finding cover, moving inside but peeking out through the windows to see what would happen. It was likely to be their biggest event of the year besides the Fourth of July. But they weren't the only ones moving. Tom Lang was barging down that boardwalk we were facing, oblivious to what else might be going on around him. He walked right past two of Watts' gunmen and crashed through those batwing doors like so many head of cattle. That sort of diverted all of us for the moment. Apparently my boys hadn't caught up to him, which made me wonder in that split second just where indeed they were.

"Fill your hand!" was all that could be heard before two six-guns went off almost simultaneously. Next there was a stream of scared men rushing out, yelling about a couple of dead men inside. Tom Lang had found Lem Cordova.

"Marshal's right, Jared," I called. "Fish or cut bait." It was the wrong thing to say. Watts' gunmen all went for their weapons.

Bud was faster that day, had his *pistolas* out in a fraction of a second, and gave one of Watts' men a one-way ticket to hell right then and there. Bud was also the first one to die on that street. Maria had been right. Watts was going to get rid of all of us, no matter how many men or how much back shooting it took. Bud had no more than gotten his shots off than he took a bullet in the back, just like his brother had. It was then that Latch Key stepped out onto the boardwalk, flattened his back against the front of the marshal's office, and brought his six-gun to bear when the killer came out of the alley way.

"Sandy," he called amongst all the other gunfire, and pulled the trigger, putting a bullet through the heart of the man Cordova had broken out of jail. Then the cook was dodging bullets just like the rest of us.

Jim Callahan wasn't as fast as Bud, but whoever it was that hired him had gotten the right man for the job. Fast isn't always the best. Accurate is what you've got to be if you want to live long enough to get fast. This Callahan lad worked real hard at making every shot count and never wasted one ounce of lead. That right hand Colt's of his planted two slugs in one gunmen's chest while the left one snaked its way out and found a target coming out of another back alley. Dug up some splinters when he shot, but they were just as good as bullets, for they went flying into the man's eye.

Another of Watts men was either running toward the man with the splintered eye or figuring on using that back alley as a retreat but never made it. It's hard missing the big body of Matthew when he's in motion and that he was, running down the boardwalk toward the gunfire. It was he that stopped the fleeing man dead in his tracks with his Winchester. Matthew was one of those people who didn't like wasting ammunition either.

The one shot I'd been able to get off in those few seconds was the one that had lifted another of Watts' gunmen up, pushing him back into a horse that kicked him before he fell. I doubt he ever felt the kick.

"Smart ass," I muttered, levering another round into my brass boy.

There was enough gunpowder filling the air to remind you of a cloud setting down around you on one of the Shinin' Mountains. Everything on my left was being taken care of in good order by Matthew, Diah, and Long John. Jim Callahan didn't have any easy look about him now. The man stood there with anger in his eyes, guns in both fists, daring any and all to potshot him. It was a matter of having a lot of guts or damn few brains, I reckon, although we didn't have time to argue about it while it was going on.

Perhaps the strangest thing about the scene was the fact that Latch Key still had on that apron of his. Let me tell you, son, that as odd as it may be, it saved his life. There was one big pocket high in the chest of the apron that he used for carrying his watch. Only today it bulged out a mite more, the bulge, it turned out, being that money he said he was going to pay back to Watts. Latch Key was stepping over the man he'd shot when another of Watts' men came out of a doorway of a store down the block and shot Latch Key full in the chest. Knocked him ass over teakettle, that shot did. It just didn't kill him like the shooter thought. Maybe it was the sound of some of those gold coins falling out of his apron that lured the man toward him, I don't know. If it was, it was damn sure the death of him. I figure the last thing he saw in this lifetime was Latch Key's six-gun coming to bear and doing the same thing to him, only twice over. Two shots and he was dead.

Long John was wounded in the arm but never stopped firing until that Winchester was empty and he had to reload. Killed two of the yahoos who were potshotting from the roof of the saloon. They didn't do it for long.

The side of my leg felt like it had been struck by a fast flying rock, knocking me off balance and to the ground.

My hand instantly found its way to my upper thigh, but I had to look quick to see what happened for I felt no blood. One hell of a bruise but no blood. The bullet had ricocheted against my bowie, shattering the blade if what I felt was correct. Still, better the knife than me.

I got to my feet right quick once a few more bullets kicked up the dirt around me. Being an open target doesn't do a hell of a lot for your health or longevity. I spotted Jared Watts milling about between the horses. It was he who had done all the big talking so far, but he was now hiding from the very people he had sworn to kill. Seeing him there like that made my blood boil and I started to half run toward him, feeling as careless as young Callahan about who was shooting at me now. Just like Tom Lang, I had a mission to perform, something I was going to do before I died. By God, I was going to see Jared Watts fry in hell!

His first shot missed me as he headed for the boardwalk and the saloon. The second one shattered the stock of my Brass Boy, but that didn't mean the firing mechanism wouldn't work. My shot was wild, just tearing at the coat he wore. The action still worked and I levered another round into the chamber, moving toward him all the time. His third shot hit me in the shoulder, feeling like it struck a bone the way it spun me around. But I was determined to get him, even as he disappeared inside the saloon. I'd likely get killed my own self doing it, but I was madder than hell and willing to risk it.

I never had to take that gamble.

I was about to charge into that saloon when I heard a shotgun blast from inside, and felt the reverberation of the discharge. I flattened myself against the wall before poking my head inside. The gunfire was dying down now and from what I saw I had a hunch I wouldn't be needing my Brass Boy any more that day. Lem Cordova and Tom Lang were there on the floor, both looking pretty dead. Jared Watts was lying in the center, half of his guts falling out of him. I knew he was dead. Holding the shotgun that had killed him was Maria, tears running down her face, her lip quivering.

"Told you I was a good shot," she said, then dropped the scatter gun and rushed into my arms, crying. Like I said, the woman was just full of surprises.

It sounded quiet as a graveyard outside, maybe because that was what it looked like. The corpses just hadn't been buried yet.

"I got a few prisoners, Black Jack," Jim Callahan said, stepping inside the batwings, "but I think one of 'em's getting away." The look on his face said that bothered him.

A distant shot rang out just then.

"No, he didn't." The deep voice barely speaking now came from Tom Lang. And once again that rare smile came to his face. "The chief, he's a good Injun."

Chapter 21

Tom Lang didn't die after all, as bloody as he looked lying on that saloon floor that day. And Jim Callahan didn't have to worry any about what he'd thought was that one man getting away. Lang had been right. In all the excitement I'd forgotten about Eagle Feather, but he hadn't forgotten about us. What he'd done was bypass the railroad, stockyards, and such and planted himself at the other end of town. He was carrying one of those Winchesters, too, and when that yahoo ran past, he put it to good use.

The only part of Jared Watts' crowd that was going back to Texas were those handful who'd had the good sense to throw in their hands before they lost the farm entirely.

The way Lang told it, after he'd called out Lem Cordova, the outlaw, who was standing at the bar, didn't even go for a gun as he faced the tall Texan. Hell, he didn't have to! The man had two six-guns lying there on the bar top and brought both of them around at the same time, the first shot hitting Lang high in the chest while the second went off the same time our trail boss was giving out some flame of his own. Cordova's second shot missed. Tom Lang's didn't. As hard hit as he was, he'd managed to put a bullet in his enemy's eye that traveled through the brain and killed him instantly. From

what Tom said later, all he remembered before falling
down his own self was seeing a part of Cordova's skull
flying out the back of his head as the air filled with more
gunsmoke.

Mad will do it every time, son. You want to be careful
of just how far it is you push someone. I'd heard tell of
miners using something new they called nitroglycerin to
blast away at those bigger mines. Powerful stuff they
were saying, but it came in a damn small bottle. The
mad in a person is the same way, believe me. What most
folks don't seem to realize is that it's the most unlikely
person who usually winds up doing one hell of a lot of
damage. Like I said, you can back water just so much
before the dam breaks. You didn't think I'd come away
from all of those years trapping beaver not knowing
something, did you?

Maria was one of those unlikely people. Had a mind
of her own, that woman. After hearing what Carl had
said about Cordova and Watts before he and Davy were
murdered, well, I reckon she'd about had her fill of
Mister Jared Watts. That was why she'd come after us
with Latch Key. But not even my harsh words could
keep her from what she had in mind. She'd heard us
speak of the most frequented saloon in town and figured
Watts would be hanging out there while his men did the
dirty work, as usual. She'd come in the back door just
after Cordova and Lang shot it out and the saloon emp-
tied out as though word of a cholera epidemic was
spreading. She'd gotten the sawed-off shotgun from behind the bar just as Jared Watts was trying to kill me and
she finally got her wish when he stumbled into the
saloon. Like I said, mad will do it every time.

I took a slug in the shoulder and cussed like hell about
it. You get shot twice in the same place, why, you tend
to notice it, hoss. Matthew and Diah had come through
the whole mess without so much as a scratch. Not that
they hadn't been pulling their own weight, mind you.
Hell, to hear them talk after the shooting was over,
they'd saved each other's lives. Each was on one side of
the street and while the marshal, Bud, Latch Key, Long

John, and I were thinning out the Watts crew, my boys were sharpshooting the roofs on each side of the street. Watts must've figured he had his bets covered with a few extra guns on the rooftops just in case things did get too fiery for him. But Matthew and Diah took care of that. Fact is that the two were actually speaking well of each other after that. Now, you want a surprise, son, why, that's it!

Whether it was foolish or brave, Jim Callahan had come through it with nothing more than a bullet hole in the side of his frock coat and a shirt with everyone else's blood on it but his own. Being shot in the chest like he was and knocked flat on his git up end was the closest Latch Key came to being harmed that day. Said he had one hell of a bruise on his chest and complained until the sun went down about his daddy's watch being busted up the way it had been. I reckon it was the marshal's comment that brought us some peace and quiet from the man.

"You ever consider the alternative, Latch Key?" he asked, that easy smile coming to him as he said it. The grizzled cook gave him a cautious look. Man reminded me of me in some ways. "Your daddy's watch is gone, but you ain't. Might be your daddy's watch served its best purpose ever today."

"Oh," was all the cook said before lapsing into silence.

Slim, Bob, Charlie, and Frank, the real cowhands of the drive, decided to stay until Tom Lang was ready to travel again. Me, I wasn't worried a lick about those prisoners they'd be taking back with them. Hell, I wasn't even concerned about the jail those gunmen would be staying in. After seeing young Callahan dealing in lead the way he had, why, I do believe he could've sat those yahoos on the porch in front of the jail and they'd have acted just like young children on good behavior.

"You remind me of another lad I run into a few years back," I said to Callahan as the boys and I readied to leave a week later. Long John and the chief had drawn their pay and would be returning to Texas with Tom Lang and his boys.

"Who's that?"

"Hickok, his name was."

"Oh, yeah." The marshal nodded, "I've heard of him. Getting a reputation for doing just about everything if half of what they say is true." He smiled modestly. "But you know how that goes."

"That I do. Been accused of it at times myself," I said.

"Why such a long look, hoss?" Jim asked Latch Key, who was seated atop the chuck wagon and looked as though he'd just downed a full quart of vinegar. I was figuring on taking that chuck wagon back to Texas with me and selling it to one of the ranchers whose money I'd also be escorting back. But seeing my cook that morning told me that the trip back might be just as bad as the trek up here had been.

"I'll tell you what it is," Diah said, taking in both Latch Key and Maria, who would be driving the supply wagon back. "He's scared to death of talking to that woman."

"What! What are you talking about?" Maria said in shock, glancing first at Diah, then at the man she'd spent most of her time working with the last three months.

"Well," the scuffy cook said, drawing it out, "I never figured you'd want a man like me. I mean, there was just that one—" We were burning daylight as it was, so I figured I'd hurry things along some.

"Why was it you were telling me you'd never got married, Maria?" I asked.

"Why, no one could ever stand up to my pa and my brothers," she replied innocently enough.

"That's all?" The cook frowned, a tad bit of fire coming to his eyes.

"Well, yeah," she shrugged. I don't think she knew what he was getting at. But it wasn't long before she found out.

Quick as a wink, he wrapped his reins around the brake of the chuck wagon, jumped down, and grabbed the reins to the supply wagon's team from the woman's hand, doing the same thing with them.

"Come on," he ordered. A look of shock came over Maria's face as she silently obeyed Latch Key. The difference was that he wasn't talking to her as though she were his cook's helper. He was a man and she was a woman and that was that. Taking her by the hand, he led her to the rear of the wagons, freeing the horse that was tied behind each. "Let's go."

"Where?" The woman was still a mite perplexed. By the time she'd asked, Latch Key was mounted.

"Fork it, lady!" he said, pointing at the saddle of the other horse. "Point that hoss to wherever it is your pa and brothers are staying. I got some talking to do to 'em and I got a notion it ain't all gonna be with words."

It struck her then what it was he had in mind. "Well, ain't that sweet," she purred like some satisfied kitten.

"Come on," the cook said, pointing once again to the empty saddle. "Fork it." This time she wasted no time in mounting up. Then the two of them lit out of there like a Comanche raiding party was after them. It wasn't the best of manners, mind you, but love does things to a man. They'd make it, those two. Besides, the cook never had gotten the chance to give Jared Watts that five hundred dollars, and Maria's past had died with him. That would give them as good a start as any.

"What're you gonna do with the wagons?" Callahan asked when the two were out of sight.

Like I said, we were burning daylight as it was, so I made a quick decision.

"Tell you what, Jim," I said, "you give Tom Lang these wagons and tell him that now he can't say I never gave him nothing but a hard time." What the hell, the wagons would only slow us down.

"You bet, Black Jack. You fellas watch your top knot and don't make yourself scarce," he said as we rode out of town.

It was a few miles out that Matthew got a curious look about him.

"Say, Pa, if we ain't got that chuck wagon and its provisions, what're we gonna do for food?" he asked.

"Why, live off the land, son, just like we always

have.'' I gave them a smile when I said it, but it didn't comfort them any. Three months on the trail, as hard as it had been, had gotten them used to some decent meals on a daily basis.

Hell, I can't help it if those prairie chickens and jack-rabbits are stringy.

About the Author

Jim Miller began his writing career at the age of ten when his uncle presented him with his first Zane Grey novel. A direct descendant of Leif Erickson and Eric the Red, and a thirteen-year army veteran, Mr. Miller boasts that stories of adventure flow naturally in his blood. His novels to date include SUNSETS, the six books in the Colt Revolver series, and the Long Guns novels: THE BIG FIFTY, MISTER HENRY, SPENCER'S REVENGE, and THE BRASS BOY.

When not busy writing about the future exploits of the Hooker men, Mr. Miller spends his time ensconced in his two-thousand-volume library filled mostly with history texts on the Old West. He lives in Aurora, Colorado, with his wife Joan and their two children.

JIM MILLER'S
SHARP-SHOOTIN'
ST⊙RIES
O' THE WAYS
O' THE WEST!!